KILLER BRIDAL PARTY

FIREFLY JUNCTION #2

LONDON LOVETT

WILD FOX PRESS

Killer Bridal Party

Copyright © 2018 by London Lovett

All rights reserved.

ISBN-13: 978-1717178923

ISBN-10: 1717178928

CHAPTER 1

*U*rsula's arms were crossed tightly as she tapped her foot impatiently at Henry. Her short, spiky hair vibrated angrily in the breeze coming down off the mountains. Henry stopped to tie his long ponytail into a knot before continuing on his task of loading his tools into the back of the truck.

I rested my feet on the porch railing and returned to my book. A tennis ball shot past my head. Newman bolted to his feet and entered one of those cartoon moments where his paws couldn't get traction. He ran in place for a second before vaulting off the porch and after the ball.

I didn't look up from my book. I wasn't sure what had me more stunned, the fact that a ghost was hanging around the house or that a hard core skeptic like myself had so easily learned to accept it.

"One day, someone is going to see that ball shoot out of nowhere and your secret will be out." I flipped to the next page.

"My secret? I have no secrets." Edward scoffed, something he was exceptionally good at. He drifted to the front edge of the porch, his boundary in the human world. He could never again walk over grass or through trees but then it wasn't like he would enjoy the feel of cool blades between his toes anyways. My overly curious mind went right into question mode. There were still so many things I needed to learn about my incorporeal house guest. (I suppose, technically, I was his house guest.) Did he even have toes? He was stuck eternally in a striking pair of black Hessian boots, so it was hard to verify. Although, he had fingers, vaporous as they were. He could grip a tennis ball with them but did he feel the ball?

The bed of the truck slammed shut, startling a cluster of mourning doves out of their afternoon food search. "I told you not to slam the truck bed like that," Ursula yelled at Henry. He ignored her, his usual response, and climbed into the truck.

"An insufferable pair of halfwits," Edward drawled as he watched the truck leave in a spray of dust. "And why does that man allow her constant crowing? And his hair, so long he has to knot it up like a nanny's bun."

"Interesting observation from a man sporting a ponytail of hair tied up with blue ribbon."

"It's called a queue and it's a timeless hairstyle for men."

I laughed. "Timeless for you maybe, but I assure you, if you were to step off this porch, you could walk from one end of town to the other and not find one man wearing a blue ribbon in his hair." I closed the book and stood next to Edward on the porch. "Ursula and Henry are entertaining, and perhaps slightly annoying. But they do good work."

"Your opinion," Edward huffed.

Newman returned and dropped the ball at the bottom of the steps.

"And you're a halfwit too, animal. I've told you to bring it up to the porch or learn to throw that blasted ball yourself."

"You are grumpy. Did you get up on the wrong side of the ghost bed? Wait. Do you have a bed?"

"Perhaps that absurd line of questioning should have started with, 'do you sleep?' Would have saved you the time of thinking up the last two."

"So you don't sleep?" I stared up at his profile. I noticed that when his emotions were strong, like now, then his image was clearer, more vibrant. His straight nose and strong chin showed a man who had been quite the vision in human form. It wasn't hard to see how Bonnie Ross, the young bride of Cleveland Ross, had fallen for him.

"Why would I need sleep? I've been at eternal rest for two centuries."

"Nope. I don't think they call your situation eternal rest. It's eternal hovering. What happens when you try and step off the porch?" I asked.

"Nothing. Nothing at all because I can't step off of it."

"So, if you do this—" I hopped down to the bottom step and turned back to him. He was watching me with that wry amused expression he wore so well. "Then you can't do this?" I crouched down for a standing broad jump and flew into the grass with a solid landing. I quickly assessed the distance I'd jumped. "Hmm, that's about nine feet. Not bad considering I haven't been on a track team since high school."

His brow arched. "That was two meters at best. Then, as a young girl you raced and jumped and, as I've noticed more than once, exercised? Hardly ladylike endeavors."

"I suppose not, but then ladylike endeavors," I said it with a snooty mimic of his posh British accent, "are not really a thing in the twenty-first century." I picked up the ball and threw it for Newman. Redford, apparently bored with the conversation on the porch, loped after him.

I climbed back up the steps and stopped to give Edward a once over. "Your grumpiness this afternoon has made your image much sharper. I have to admit, although I'll probably regret it, you must have been quite stunning in flesh and blood form."

"Naturally. Good breeding and all that. I was told that I was related to distant royalty."

"Oh really? Bonnie Prince Charlie?"

He hesitated and his face faded away for a second, something I'd seen him do on occasion when he wasn't anxious to answer one of my million questions. I'd noticed it mostly when I brought up uncomfortable topics. "Richard the third," he said quickly, apparently hoping the answer would float away on a breeze.

I covered my mouth to stifle a laugh. "Wasn't he terribly unpopular? And wasn't he the guy whose spine was curved so badly—"

"Yes," he snapped to end my question. "He had a few character and physical flaws, it's true. But the point is, are you related to royalty?"

"Actually, that's not really the point at all, but if we're going to be technical, my mom won the title of Homecoming Queen at her school dance. So there's that."

Edward, of course, had no idea what a homecoming queen was and I was just as glad not to tell him since it would only earn me an eye roll and follow-up lecture about the quaint, mundane traditions of modern American life.

"There's Emily." I waved to my sister as she came across the pasture that stretched between the Cider Ridge Inn and her adorable farm several acres away. Emily was the only member of the family blessed with my Great Aunt Rhonda's naturally golden hair and blue eyes. I'd managed to get the blue eyes but my hair was a dark brown, a color that I found irritatingly non-descript. It wasn't a rich coffee color or a tawny-toffee tan. It was just brown.

A basket filled with Emily's organic eggs, spinach and tomatoes swung at her side as she hiked through the grass in her white cut-off shorts and green tank top. The mid summer sun had brought a day filled with a nice dose of heat and a little too much humidity.

But Emily always looked cool and collected, no matter how sweltering the temperature.

"More spinach," Edward noted. "You eat as many greens as a—"

"Watch how you end that analogy," I advised.

"Rabbit," he said confidently.

"Good choice." I peered up at him. It was strange to think that I was standing next to him, conversing with him, even exchanging barbs, only no one else could see him but me. More than once, the terrifying thought had occurred to me that he wasn't there at all and that Edward Beckett was a figment of my off-the-charts, crazy imagination. But then he'd do something sneaky, like move Ursula's tape measure for amusement and I'd know he was actually there. Or was he *there*? I couldn't really find a word to describe his presence.

Edward was staring out at the pasture.

"If you have complete control over who can see and hear you, why did you reveal yourself to me?" It was such an obvious question, yet I had never thought to ask it.

"I thought I made that clear."

I crossed my arms and turned to him. "No, not really."

He turned and the way he stood, with one boot crossed over the other made it look as if he was leaning casually against some invisible post. "Have you forgotten that you attempted to paint the sitting room—what was that ridiculous color—yes, Cupid Pink?"

"I'll admit the gray you helped me choose was much more elegant. But that can't be the only reason you decided to introduce yourself."

"Like you've so aptly put it, I need to find out what's been keeping me in-between worlds, and I thought you seemed smart."

"Did you?"

"Well, relatively so. Except the pink fiasco."

Emily reached the yard. "My youngest sister is the beauty of the family," I said without moving my lips, so Emily wouldn't notice me talking.

"I think you're wrong on that assessment too. Just like the pink." It was hard to read exactly what he meant, but I had no time to decipher it.

I smiled probably just a little too enthusiastically at my sister.

Emily looked around the porch and took a soft, deep breath. She even managed to look pretty while out of breath. "Who were you talking to, sis?"

"Huh? Oh, Redford and Newman."

Naturally, my dogs came bounding across the field at the sound of their names and the sight of their favorite person, Emily.

"There you boys are." She reached for the treats in her pocket. "Your mommy was talking to herself and trying to put the blame on you, but we'll keep her little secret." She tossed them her home-made peanut butter dog cookies, and they trotted off to a shady spot to eat them. "Are you ready to walk to Lana's?"

"I am." I looked briefly back. Edward was no longer standing on the porch. Maybe he was just a figment of my imagination after all.

CHAPTER 2

*E*mily's husband had gone into town to meet some friends for a beer so Emily, Lana, Raine and I planned a girls' night in Lana's kitchen. We decided to make Spanish omelets with fresh goodies from Emily's farm. Raine's old Volkswagen was parked in front of the barn, which meant Lana and Raine were still working on something for the party business. There was a silver sedan parked next to Raine's car. Lana had mentioned that a bride-to-be was stopping by to help with shower party treat bags and to pick a place setting for her wedding.

Redford and Newman loped ahead to let them know we'd arrived.

"How are Tinkerbell and Cuddlebug? Have they been asking about Aunt Sunni?" At the start of summer, Emily had adopted two baby goats. I'd been going out of my way to show up at bottle feeding time just so I could sit and watch their cute little muzzles tug at the rubber nipple. I had multiple photos of both goats with milk moustaches from feeding time. Whenever I needed a smile or laugh, I pulled up the pictures.

"As a matter of fact, Tink was asking just this morning 'where's the crazy lady who can't stop hugging me and who keeps taking my picture?'"

"Guilty as charged."

Up ahead, Lana appeared at the wide entrance to her party barn to give the dogs a treat. The late afternoon sun glinted off the white oak siding. For parties and weddings, Lana transformed the clean, well-kept barn into a showpiece, inside and out.

"Between the two of you giving out treats so freely, Redford and Newman are going to look like hippos instead of Border Collies."

Emily motioned toward the sedan. "I guess the bride is still making her selections. Lana said she was putting together the bridal shower for her too. It sounds fun. It's a camping trip in the mountain park. I guess it's called glamping, still outdoors but with some indoor comforts."

"Lana mentioned that to me too. I found it interesting that the bride was able to get all her guests on board for a night out in the mountains. Especially old aunts and grandmothers who might have left their outdoorsy days behind."

"From what Lana told me, they had a special shower for the people who weren't interested in a night under the stars. This one will be just for her adventurous friends."

We reached the barn. Raine looked up from the work table where she was filling red bandanas with small bottles of hand lotion, sparkly little flashlights, trail mix and other goodies for an overnight satchel. A dozen or so finished 'bandana gift bags' were tied to the ends of sticks like a hobo's knapsack.

"Hey, guys, we're almost done here." Raine pushed her black-rimmed glasses higher on her nose and eyed the basket in Emily's hand. "Can't wait for dinner. My tyrannical boss hasn't given me a break all afternoon." She pointed out the tray of mason jars at the end of the table. Each jar contained marshmallows, chocolate squares and graham crackers for S'mores. Lana and Raine had hand-painted pale blue polka dots on the silver lids and a name was neatly painted along the side of each jar.

Lana winked at us over the heads of her client and friends as the three women surveyed the table settings my sister had laid out.

My talented older sister had arranged three styles of place settings, ranging from elegant to rustic. The first option was made up of a clear glass charger beneath two ivory plates both rimmed with gold. The utensils were gold plated and a thin band of gold lined the rim of the stemmed glassware. The stack of plates was bound by a pale blue satin bow. It seemed pale blue was the primary wedding color because each place setting had some splash of the pastel color. The second setting, my favorite, consisted of a pale blue dinner plate topped by a scroll edged gold and white salad plate. They were stacked atop an ornate silver charger with matching silver utensils. A pink rose and white linen napkin bound by a pearl band finished off the look. The third setting would have been Emily's choice, a mahogany wood charger with a white and black plate and pale blue linen napkins. The napkin rings were sprigs of laurel.

Lana, who was always the supreme hostess, had placed out a snack tray of chips, veggies and dip for the women to snack on while they made their extremely important decision.

Emily set down her basket of produce and eggs, and we both got to work helping Raine fill the bandana knapsacks. It was easy to spot which of the women was the bride because she was the center of everyone's attention. Lana included. She was a feathery thin woman whose head was slightly too big for her body. I knew women tended to lose weight for their 'big day', but this particular bride might have taken things too far. Although, her cheeks were a rosy pink and not sallow like one might expect from a crash diet and she wasn't shy with the chips and dip that Lana had set out. It was more than possible that she had just been one of those waifish thin people her entire life. She, like many future brides, seemed to revel in the idea of being the center of the world. She nearly bit through her lip, trying to pick the right place setting, which was partly my sister's fault. Each of the example settings would look lavish and breathtaking on the reception tables. It was a hard choice to make.

"Brooke Lewis, the bride, is the bone thin woman who keeps chewing on her lip," Raine whispered.

I leaned closer and spoke quickly. "Is the maid of honor the fast moving woman who seems to be making all the suggestions and comments and who looks to be taking this all quite seriously?"

Emily poked me with her elbow for being so judgmental.

Raine glanced back to make sure they were out of earshot. "Yes," she said in a loud whisper. "That's Tory Jansen and you've probably already noticed that she has no love for the other brides-maid, Cindy Hargrove."

I looked past Raine but kept my bold stare hidden. The second friend had shiny dark hair that was cut stylishly short. She had large, expressive eyes and a turned up nose that looked better from the side than from the front. She also seemed to be a nervous laugher, someone who giggled spontaneously at everything the bride said. It seemed nothing was too trite or mundane for her mirth. Either that, or she was badly trying to make herself the favorite bridesmaid. And Raine was exactly right. As much as she smiled and laughed at everything Brooke said, she produced a scowl for her bridesmaid partner's remarks.

"I see it too." Emily had relented and joined in on the gossip session. Something she rarely did. "The two bridesmaids seem totally at odds with each other. Maybe it's because Tory is maid of honor."

Raine shook her head discretely and leaned in. "Or it might be that Cindy is still holding a grudge from high school when Tory stole Cindy's prom date, Matthew Bigelow, right out from under her turned up nose."

"How do you know all this?" I accidentally stuck two flashlights into one knapsack and was immediately admonished with a tongue click.

Raine took out the extra flashlight and set it aside. "I went to high school with them. I can't believe they all stayed friends."

"All right then." Lana sounded relieved a decision had been made. "We'll go with the rose setting in the middle. Now there's still about a week's time if you change your mind," Lana said as she escorted them out.

"No, don't tell her that," Cindy said with an extra dose of laughter. "She'll be changing her mind every day for a week."

Apparently, the maid of honor thought the comment was unnecessary and made a point of rolling her eyes in response. Brooke made a point of hugging each friend to thank them for helping her decide, and that produced smiles all around.

Brooke smiled our direction and my sister quickly introduced us. Before leaving, she walked over to look at the knapsacks. "Oh, Lana, these are perfect. My guests will love them. Raine, I was thinking of having my palm read before the wedding. Just for fun, you know."

Raine's lips flattened at the notion that her palm reading was *just for fun*. She took her psychic abilities very seriously and considered herself an expert medium who could converse with the spirit world. I had to push back a grin at that thought. If she only knew.

"Sure. Stop in tomorrow before noon. I'll be out here working with Lana after that."

"Terrific," Brooke said. "See you then."

Lana walked them out and spent a few minutes chatting before returning. "I think she's going to regret having both of those women in her wedding party." Lana picked up a carrot stick and dipped it.

I decided to do the same, only my veggie of choice was a round red radish. "They seemed to be shooting daggers at each other with their eyes every time the bride looked away."

"Yes." Lana started picking up the plates and silverware. I pitched in a hand to help. "Brooke has invited all four of her bridesmaids up to the campsite tomorrow night so they can have one night of fun before the shower guests arrive on Saturday. She's hoping it'll be a night of bonding, but I'm not so sure. And what she doesn't know is that the male half of the wedding party is planning to show up and surprise them while they're sitting around the campfire."

"That could be good or bad," I said as I followed her to the plate boxes.

"That's what I was thinking. I tried to talk the groom out of the idea, but he's sure it will be a great surprise. He's one of those confident, know-it-all types. His family owns Stockton Tools, the biggest toolmaker on this side of the country. Jeremy is apparently the heir to the tool throne. Tory, the maid of honor, is one of their lead salespeople. Anyhow, I sure could use your help setting up the camping party tomorrow afternoon."

"Sure. I can get away from the newspaper office early. Maybe a night under the stars, surrounded by lightning bugs and the cooing sounds of nature will bring harmony to the bridal party."

Raine laughed. "Of course, because sleeping on the uncomfortable ground, swatting at mosquitoes and having to hike to the portable potties always brings out the best in people."

CHAPTER 3

*L*ana's kitchen was one of our favorite gathering spots. Emily and I had stationed ourselves at the long maple table under the cluttered pot rack and pendant lights. Emily was chopping tomatoes for a salsa to go with the omelet, and I was making myself useful cutting limes for some margaritas.

Lana had tied on a cute black and white plaid apron. She was stirring up a bowl of eggs and cream. "I think you should get a few cows for the farm, Em. Then we could have fresh cream."

"And butter," I added enthusiastically.

Emily swept a pile of tomato chunks into a bowl. "Sunni, you do realize that butter doesn't flow naturally from the cow?"

"No? Maybe someone should breed cows who produce butter." I piled up my limes. "I'd be willing to churn it, if you're willing to take care of the cows."

Raine was frying up some onions. "Fresh butter would be tasty. Who am I kidding? Butter in any form is tasty. Even those silly butter shaped turkeys they sell near Thanksgiving."

I poured margaritas from the blender and topped them with

my very professionally cut limes. I handed Raine her glass, which she desperately needed after working over the hot stove. She took a sip. "Hmm, well done, my friend. Hey, how are *things* at the inn?" Raine and I had become quick friends after I moved to Firefly Junction. We were very different but we got along well. Sometimes it was nice having a confidante around who wasn't a sister. My sisters were my true best friends, but they were also family.

"If by your special pronunciation of the word *things*, you mean unusual, unexplained events, then all is well and normal at the inn." Edward insisted that no one else know about his existence. He didn't want reporters and ghost hunters swarming the inn, which was the height of irony considering my occupation. But I'd agreed to it. Especially because he also assured me that he would never corroborate my claims by making himself visible or obvious, which would, in turn, make me appear daft. (His word, not mine.) But not being able to tell, of all people, Raine, the professed medium and bridge to the spirit world, was exceptionally hard. Otherwise, I was perfectly fine not revealing my secret to anyone. It was a secret that was frankly a little too baffling to explain.

Raine turned off the stove. "Onions are done, Lana." Raine turned to me. "That's not what I hear from Ursula and Henry. Ursula told me tools and things get mysteriously moved and she's sure she occasionally hears someone laughing."

"Please, Raine, if you're going to take Ursula's word over mine, then there's nothing I can say. Let me just remind you that Ursula lectured and whined about her missing hammer for a week before she ended up finding it in her tool box. The woman gets worked up if Henry slurps his soup too loud. Everything in her world is over-the-top and hyperbolic."

I delivered a drink to Lana, who winked at me over the brim before taking a sip. She was a skeptic like me, only I was no longer a skeptic. I wasn't sure what the word was for someone who was still having a hard time believing something that was right in front of them.

"But Henry agrees with Ursula that something funny is going on." Raine hadn't given up yet. But that was hardly surprising. I'd allowed her one night of a séance, before I learned that there actually was a spirit hanging around the inn. But the séance had produced nothing. In fact, after spending some time with my somewhat transparent house mate, I was certain Edward had sat right there in that room, watching the entire spectacle for his amusement. Couldn't blame him really. The inn had been vacant for years and he'd been left to wander the halls alone all that time, stuck in his holding cell between worlds. He must have been bored silly.

"What are you working on for the paper?" Emily piped up from her salsa making task. She was carefully pulling cilantro leaves off the stems. Emily knew that Raine could dwell on things and we probably needed a subject change.

"Now that you ask—" I enthusiastically pulled out a chair and sat down with my citrusy margarita. "Remember when I told you about the strange, unexplained death of a lot of fish and frogs in the river?"

"Yes." Emily chopped the cilantro. "Did you find the source?"

"As a matter of fact I did. A few of the locals who like to fish at a certain pool along the river told me that the silt in the river, even after a storm, looked grainy instead of muddy."

"Grainy?" Lana asked. "Like sand?"

I took a sip of my drink and puckered my mouth at the sourness. "No, I mean like grain from plants. I went to the fishing hole and saw that they were right. I could see flecks of seeds and rice-like grain in the dirt. I scooped up a sample and had it analyzed. It turned out to be the spent grain from a brewery. The evidence sent me right to the culprit. Only they had no idea they were culprits or that they were doing anything wrong."

Emily held up her finger for me to pause. She flipped the switch on the blender, and the tomato and onion chunks morphed into a rich red salsa. She turned off the blender and waved her hand for me to continue.

"Smoky's Craft Beer is a local, homegrown brewery started by a few fresh out of college grads. They recently opened the doors to expanded production after they landed some solid contracts with local beer distributors. Anyhow, as I learned during my research, beer production leaves behind a lot of waste, especially in spent grains. Since the waste was all organic material, the brewers thought they could drop it in piles along the river as a sort of offering to the local wildlife. But every time it rained, the river rose up and swept the debris downstream. Apparently the fish were eating way too much of it. On top of that, the extra solids in the river were clogging up ecosystems and stealing oxygen."

"Wow, my sister saved the river. Good for you, Sunni." Emily poured her salsa into a bowl.

Lana spun around from her task. "But what about the brewery? Won't the negative press hurt them?" My sisters were so predictable. Emily was siding with the critters reliant on the river ecosystem, and Lana's empathy went straight to the business owners.

"Fortunately, my article is two-fold with two happy endings. One that will satisfy my animal and earth loving sister." I held up my drink toward Emily. "And one that will satisfy my profit loving sister." I toasted my drink toward Lana.

Raine tilted her head at me. "What about my happy ending? Oh wait. We'd need to do a séance for that."

"Yep, sorry, the article only has the dual happy ending. No other world entities involved."

Emily tasted the salsa and seemed pleased with her accomplishment but went for a dash more salt. "I've heard that those spent grains from breweries can be used to feed cattle and pigs."

I pointed at her. "I'm way ahead of you. Naturally, when I traced the source of the problem to the brewery, they were quite upset. They had no idea they were creating a problem for the fish. They've offered to pay for a clean-up and to have the river restocked with the trout that people like to catch. I did some research and found out exactly what Emily just mentioned. I put the brewery in contact with some nearby cattle ranchers. They were happy to accept the spent grain. They are even going to pick it up every other week. So, all's well in the river ecosystem and craft brew world again. I'm just putting some polishing touches on the article before sending it to the editor. Hopefully Parker will like it."

"He seems to like all your work," Lana noted. "Maybe someday that silly man will realize that you are much more of an asset to the *Junction Times* than his top reporter, Chase Evans."

Raine walked over with a spoon to try the salsa. "That won't happen until Chase breaks it off with the newspaper owner's daughter. And since he won't find a better job, I don't think that will happen anytime soon."

I sipped some more margarita. "Lana, definitely don't mix up any drinks for that bridal party. The tequila is making us catty. And from the cold vibes transferring back and forth between the two bridesmaids earlier in the barn, I don't think they need any fuel for the fire."

"No tequila for this glamping trip," Lana said. "But at least you found something exciting to write about. I know you were fretting about the lack of scandal and intrigue in Firefly Junction."

"It's a good story, but I'd still love a good scandal to really set my investigative hair on fire. Maybe someday soon."

CHAPTER 4

$\mathcal{M}$y fingers were flying over the keyboard, and while there was no way to see his image in my monitor or feel him breathing on me, I knew Edward was looking over my shoulder reading my article about the brewery.

Edward's deep laugh rumbled through the kitchen, where I 'd set up my laptop and put on a pot of coffee to counteract the two margaritas.

"Why does that laugh sound like a lead in to a critique about my work?"

"Not at all." Edward flashed to the opposite side of the table. He picked up an apple from the bowl. I waited with mild curiosity to see just exactly what he planned to do with a piece of fruit he couldn't eat. He tossed it from hand to hand in a low level attempt at juggling.

I looked across the kitchen to the brick hearth where Newman and Redford had plopped down to wait for me to head in to bed. Newman was too tired to notice the apple being tossed back and forth like a tennis ball.

"I just find it interesting that dropping a few piles of grain along the shore of a river, a perfectly acceptable thing to do, would create such an uproar that the local journalist felt compelled to write about it."

I collapsed my fingers over the keyboard and stared up at him. It was late and the lights in the kitchen were shining through his image. "So glad you kept the biting critique out of your observation."

"You're welcome."

"Did they have sarcasm back in the early nineteenth century?"

"Sarcasm?" He reached for an orange and added it to his fruit juggle. He was fairly adept at it considering his hands were vapor.

"Never mind. And the brewery did damage to the river. Besides, it's against the law. You can't just dump debris, even if it's organic material, into a protected body of water. It damages the ecosystem, then the plants and animals die."

Edward was temporarily focused on his juggling act.

"Fine, if the discussion is over, could you take your fruit practice to another room. I'm tired and I need to finish." I dropped my face to continue typing. The fruit landed in the bowl with two successive thuds.

Edward floated up to the kitchen counter and stretched out on his side. He leaned on one transparent elbow. "In my day, every drop of waste, even substances I can not elaborate on in front of a lady, was poured into the Thames River. The Thames is a vast river that flows through London."

"Yes, I know what the Thames is. The world is a much smaller place since *your day*."

His dark brows bunched together. "The world has shrunk?"

"No, not in the physical sense." I shook my head. I was too tired to explain my metaphorical phrase. "I think the Thames is a perfect example of why my article is so important. The people living near the Thames took it for granted and thought it was so large it could never truly reach its capacity on waste. But in the mid twentieth century, the river was declared dead."

Edward laughed. "How can a river die?"

"It was so filled with pollution and bacteria it could no longer support life. So, in essence, it was just a dead body of water. But with some good laws and a massive clean-up effort, it's now considered one of the cleanest rivers in Europe."

Edward sat up. For someone who had no aches and pains or muscles to stretch or anxiety to relieve, he was certainly a restless ghost. "How do you know so much about England? It's miles of land and sea away from this place."

"As I said, the world is a much smaller place." I pointed at my computer. "I can travel to England with a touch of my finger." More and more, I realized that Edward had lived inside the inn like someone trapped in a time capsule. Outside the crumbling walls of the Cider Ridge Inn, the world continued on its path toward technology and innovation. But inside the house, Edward was stuck back in a different time. He'd told me about another owner in the mid-nineteenth century, Mary Richards, who he'd revealed himself to but he kept mostly to himself after that. Until me.

"I've watched you many times on that metal box. I'm amazed at how easily it keeps your attention."

"Yes, well." I felt slightly embarrassed about his comment. "It's possible I spend far too much time staring at the thing, but most of it is for work. Although, not all of it. Occasionally, I do get side-tracked by something mindless and enjoyable. But I assure you, I'm not the only person who spends too much time on the computer." It seemed I was tired. I was making excuses for being a part of the modern world.

The words on my screen were starting to look like one big blur. I saved the file and closed the laptop.

"Don't let me stop you from working," Edward said.

"Too late for that." I leaned back and stared at him. His cravat was always loose, and his boots were forever polished. And since his image was stuck in time, he was forever young and handsome. I thought about his reference to the Thames River. "What exactly was it that made you leave England?"

His dark gaze faded some, and his features nearly erased.

"Oh, I see, we've stepped into personal territory. I already know your family sent you off because you were a troublemaker."

My teasing words prodded him back into full view. Which was my goal.

"Trouble is a vague word. I personally think there were other more nefarious forces at work behind my banishment from the family estate."

"More nefarious? Like what?"

"A cousin who stood to gain a great deal of wealth with my removal from the family."

I sat forward, intrigued by this new plot line. "So, with you gone, this cousin inherited the family estate?"

"Yes, cousin Charles, a witless fool who was as useless as he was stupid. And that's the highest praise I could give the man."

"No question how you felt about Charles then. Maybe that's why you're sticking around. They say some unresolved issue keeps spirits from finding peace. Usually it's no resolution for a murder or a spurned lover. But we know how you died and you mentioned that your attachment to Bonnie was only of a—" I cleared my throat. "A physical nature. And thank you for sparing me details with that vague phrase. What if you're still around because you died knowing that witless Charles was living high and mighty in what was rightfully your position in society?"

"Well thought out conclusion," Edward said as he floated down from the counter.

"Really? Bully for me then." I carried my cup of coffee to the sink.

"Yes, it's a grand theory, but it's wrong."

I placed the cup in the sink and turned around. "How do you know? Do some soul searching or whatever you do when you're vapor?"

"I don't need to search my vapor," he said pointedly. "Charles died a year after I reached America. Gout or stupidity or cowardice or some other malady suffered by a rich, fat, overindulgent fool." He waved his hand. Sometimes, a gesture like the wave of his hand would appear in slow motion stretching his long white fingers to impossible lengths before the image tightened back up to regular human proportions.

"Then there was no heir to your family's estate?"

"If I had lived, it would have fallen to me. But there were a number of other greedy cousins waiting in line to be next. Of course, by the time I realized I was no longer of sound mind or solid body, the family estate was no longer important. And that is why your conclusion is wrong."

"You don't need to put extra emphasis on the word *wrong*. Got it. You're not here because you lost your family fortune to spoiled cousin Charles." A yawn crept up. I covered my mouth. "I guess we'll have to continue this another time. I'm too tired to think anymore."

"I bid you good night then."

The dogs rose groggily to their feet. Their claws clattered on the kitchen floor as they walked like sleepy children toward the bedroom. I stopped before heading down the narrow hallway.

"So you were sent to America, not because you were shaming the family name with your behavior, but because cousin Charles was plotting against you?"

Edward's image grew thin and watery. "There might have been a few instances of scandalous affairs and gambling debts. And then there was the threat of blackmail. You should go to bed. You get unsightly dark rings under your eyes when you're tired." With that confession and unflattering remark, he vanished.

I plodded with heavy feet down the hallway. Newman had already settled himself in the center of the bed, once again leaving me with just a crescent shaped mattress edge. But I didn't care. I was tired. Even more so than usual. Who knew life with a ghost would be so exhausting?

CHAPTER 5

*M*yrna had put her black hair up in a bun. She'd brushed the natural streak of white hair up from her forehead into a swirl that reminded me of the twirls on a vanilla ice cream cone. Myrna, the newspaper office manager, and I had grown instantly close and I always looked forward to seeing her smiling face when I walked into work.

Recently, she'd toned down her heavy makeup with a lighter foundation, and pink rather than cherry red lipstick. From what I gathered, the new pastels were her summer color choices. She looked up briefly from her computer and grinned. "I brought some of those donut holes with the rainbow sprinkles you like so much." Sometimes I wondered if I was so fond of the woman because I missed my mom. Myrna was only ten years older than me, but she stood in as a perfect surrogate. She always provided me with snacks and occasionally straightened up my desk when I let it get too out of control.

"Donut holes are the perfect way to start my morning." I walked over to my desk and pulled my laptop out of its case.

Parker had insisted on buying me a desktop computer, but I still preferred my laptop. Myrna had placed five rainbow sprinkled donut holes on a paper napkin in the center of my desk. I popped one into my mouth and gave her a thumbs up across the room.

I finished the overlarge bite of food and reached for one more. "I wonder how many of these donut holes equal a whole donut," I mused as I opened my computer.

"I'm sure ten or twelve," Myrna said matter-of-factly, even though she'd just pulled the numbers from thin air.

"I like the way you calculate your donut holes, lady. Then this plate is only half a donut. I wonder if the same ratio works for those mini candy bars we hand out on Halloween." As I pondered the next important question, the door to Parker's office opened. Chase Evans, the head reporter, walked out wearing a snow white Polo shirt and a palmful too much hair product. His strong, clean shaven jaw looked tight as steel, signaling he wasn't pleased about something.

He stopped at Myrna's desk and helped himself to a mint. "Can't believe I'm stuck with covering the local elections. Might as well be covering the local funerals." He stopped his short rant long enough to notice that I was in the cluttered newspaper office. "Sunni, didn't see you hiding there behind your laptop." He pasted on his dazzling smile. As picture perfect as the man was, like a glossy photo from a magazine, I found him lacking in personality, which, in turn, took away a lot of the shine. I knew the look he was wearing. He needed a favor.

"Hey, Sunni, this assignment seems right up your alley." He held up the manila folder, Parker's primitive, almost childish, system of handing out assignments. "How about you cover this—"

"She can't cover the elections," Parker growled from the doorway of his office. He'd recently decided to dye his bushy gray moustache a dark brown. It was hard not to stare at the thing.

Myrna and I had secretly decided it looked as if a fluffy mouse had climbed onto his lip and died there under his nose.

"Get in here, Taylor," Parker ordered gruffly and then cleared his throat and lightened his tone. "I've got a new assignment for you." After several successful articles, Parker had grown more confident with my reporting. While he tried to act like the tough, salty editor, there was always an edge of pride when he talked to me.

"If it's more interesting than the elections, then that assignment should go to me. I'm head reporter." Chase sounded a bit whiny, like a kid who didn't get to lead the line in from recess.

"It is more interesting than the elections." Parker's dead mouse moustache shifted back and forth a moment as if the poor critter had been jolted back to life. I was certain Chase's spoiled boy plea had done the trick and that Parker would hand me the election assignment. Chase was, after all, dating the newspaper owner's daughter. I braced for the disappointment, hoping at the very least that some scandalous candidate was running, when Parker motioned me into the office. I glanced back. Chase's mouth dropped in disbelief as Parker swung the door shut behind us.

With some effort and a few grunts, Parker settled himself down behind his desk. His usual array of vitamins, aspirin and lozenge wrappers made a nice medicinal frame around the clutter on his desk. I had to mentally remind myself not to stare at the stark brown fluff of hair above his lip. His hair was still mostly gray, which made the moustache color experiment that much more striking.

Parker mumbled to himself something about checking car brakes as he read off one of the many yellow sticky notes he had pasted around his workspace and along the edge of his computer monitor. "Here it is." He pulled a note off the top of the sticky note pad. "Gina wanted me to ask if your sister has ever done a sweet sixteen party? Our daughter's birthday is coming up next month."

"Oh, um I'm not sure, but Lana can make any party match the occasion. I've got some of her business cards on my desk." I stared at the sticky note in his hand. "Was that all you needed from me or was there an assignment?"

He blew a laugh from his mouth and the dead mouse twittered. "Yes, there's an assignment." He ruffled through a pile of folders and grabbed one out, holding it just out of my reach. "How is that article about the brewery coming along?"

"It'll be in your inbox before I leave work today."

"Great. Looking forward." He dropped the folder in front of me, causing my hair to blow back off my face. "I don't know if you've driven across the Colonial Bridge often, but it's in desperate need of restoration and repair."

"I've driven over it a number of times, and I confess, I hold my breath as I cross it."

"Right. The improvements were voted on and ratified months ago, but there hasn't been any progress. In order to save money, the city council decided to allow private companies to invest in the restoration. I've listed a few businesses that have a financial interest in the project. It might be a place to start."

I opened the folder. Parker's assignment folders were always comically scant. This one was no different. The folder consisted of one printed paper with a few company names and contact phone numbers. The title Colonial Bridge Restoration was printed boldly across the top of the paper. I drew my finger along the list. It ended with the one company I'd heard of, which was sheer coincidence. "Stockton Tools," I read out loud.

"Yes, do you know the Stocktons?"

"Only through my sister. Well, not exactly. Lana is planning the wedding for the owner's son and his bride." I closed the folder. "I'll get started on this just as soon as I finish up the details on the brewery article." I headed out of the office.

Myrna motioned me over to her desk with the crook of her

finger. I leaned down to hear her hushed voice. "Chase is so mad," she whispered.

I quickly glanced into the newsroom.

"He went out to meet Rebecca for coffee," Myrna said in her usual easy to hear tone. She patted a notepad that was covered with her speedy shorthand. "I just got a wedding announcement. Apparently Jeremy Stockton of Stockton Tools is getting married to a local girl." She looked at her notes to find the name.

"Brooke Lewis," I filled in for her. "Lana is putting on the reception up at the barn."

"I bet it will be beautiful. The Stocktons are a well-respected family in these parts," Myrna continued. "Joseph Stockton started that company about eighty years ago." She grinned and moved closer as if she had another juicy piece of gossip. "My Grandmother Gertie dated Joseph for a few months until he joined the army. She couldn't be bothered to wait for him to return and married my grandfather, a wonderful man but not nearly as rich and successful as Joseph Stockton." She shifted back to her computer, a signal that she'd divulged all the gossip tidbits for the time being.

I walked back to my desk. There was a text from Raine. "Lunch after I read the bride-to-be's fortune?"

I texted back. "Yes. I'll need to eat something healthy after my donut hole overload. See you at noon."

CHAPTER 6

*R*aine's shop was just blocks away from the newspaper office. I'd spent the morning nibbling donut holes and finishing the brewery article and was in need of a hearty lunch. I was thinking of ordering the Charlie Chaplin at Layers, our favorite lunch spot. The Chaplin had chunks of roasted chicken smothered in smoky cheddar and tucked into a sourdough roll. It made my mouth water just to think about it. I was pleased with myself for making my choice so easily. Ballad Winter, the owner of Layers, had created such a diverse and appetizing menu, I found that if I didn't decide before walking into the restaurant, I risked using up my entire lunch break reading the menu. With my choice made, I could avoid the menu altogether and save myself the anguish of indecision.

A sparkling green Jaguar was parked in front of Junction Psychic. Raine's chalkboard sign was hanging on the door. She hung it out to let people know she was in consultation with a client. I wandered over to the side yard outside of her shop where a pair of sparrows were busy splashing in the birdbath. I moved with the quiet stealth of a cat and pulled my phone free from my pocket. I was determined to catch the cute birds in the midst of their afternoon bath. I lifted the phone and moved ever so slightly to capture them both in one frame. I moved my finger slowly to the button. The view through the finder was going to be an Instagram sensation. Before I could snap the shot, the front door whisked open, and my feathered models shot up to a nearby tree.

"Darn it." It seemed my Instagram stardom was still out of reach. I pushed my phone back into my pocket and turned around.

I immediately recognized the first person out the door. It was Brooke. She was holding her mouth as if to stifle a sob as her thin legs carried her down the front steps. Her skin was pale, like it had been dusted with powder, only I was sure that was not the case. Something had caused her a great deal of despair, and whatever it was, it had washed the color right out of her complexion. The bridesmaid, Cindy, followed quickly after Brooke, shaking her head in angry disbelief. A few sharp words shot from the house and were quickly followed by the bride's grim faced, tight lipped maid of honor, Tory. Raine's face appeared next in the open doorway. She looked nearly as pale as the bride. Her anguished gaze found me standing in the shadows of the yard. Her eyes widened, letting me know she had something to tell me. But it didn't take an investigative journalist to discover that.

Tory threw her arm around Brooke's bony shoulders and quietly spoke to her as she led her to the Jaguar. Cindy opened the passenger door for Brooke and then climbed into the backseat while Tory walked around to the driver's side. She skewered Raine with an angry glare before disappearing inside. The tires on the Jag screamed and left a smoky, rubbery film in the air as they drove away.

I finally crawled out from my semi-hiding spot. "What on earth have you done, Raine? That bride-to-be looked much happier last night when she was picking out her place setting." I climbed up the steps.

"Ugh, the wedding. Your sister is going to be so mad." An array of bangles and bracelets clattered on Raine's arm as she rubbed her face. Some of the color returned to her cheeks. The wild colors of her skirt trailed a rainbow through the air as she turned back to the house with a dramatic flounce.

I followed her inside. Even though the sun was shining brightly outside the small, old house, the front room where all the psychic consultation took place had the heavy curtains shut tight. A few candles sent flickering light and a good deal of acrid smoke through the snug, heavily decorated room. There were four chairs sitting around the small table in the middle of the room. A stack of Raine's tarot cards were hastily piled next to a tea cup that was drained of liquid but covered in wet tea leaves.

"What a morning," Raine muttered as she swept up the cards into a stack.

"What happened? What did you tell her?"

"Only the truth." Raine shook her head as if she was trying to shake off the last few minutes. She busied herself extinguishing candles and putting the room back into regular order.

"Raine, you're avoiding eye contact. What truth?" I'd just placed myself in a tough predicament by asking her 'what truth'. Raine firmly believed in her skills. If I questioned what she considered to be the likely future events, then I would hurt her feelings. But how fair was it for her to upset her customers with predictions she was basing solely on her tarot cards, tea leaves and her own unwavering confidence?

Raine disappeared into the kitchen. Seconds later, the tea cup clattered into the sink. I didn't need to see it, to know the cup was no longer in one piece. Raine's string of swear words ushering out from the kitchen solidified that conclusion.

Raine returned from the kitchen and sat down hard on the

velvet settee in the corner of the room.

"I know you pride yourself on giving it to people straight, but maybe when you are sensing bad news, you should tone it down or pillow it with something good."

Raine pulled off the scarf she had tied around her head. "Oh trust me, I pillow. I pillow every chance I get. I hate when I get strong vibes about bad news, but there is almost always some inkling of good with it. Silver linings here and there, moments of good fortune that seem destined to follow bad luck."

Raine was unusually shaken by it all.

I sat next to her on the settee. "What was it that you sensed or predicted? Is the marriage in trouble?"

She rested her head back and took off her glasses. "It wasn't one particular thing. I had gooseflesh up and down my arms almost the second they walked inside, long before I laid out the cards or brewed the tea." Raine lifted her head. "I don't have the heart to tell Lana. She was excited to get this job. The Stocktons have big influence in this area, lots of connections. She saw this as a great opportunity for more referrals." Raine sat forward with a grunt. "Lana's going to kill me."

"No, I think you're reading too much into this."

"I don't think so." Raine was almost always an optimist. It was the reason people came to her for palm readings and the reason this particular incident was so distressing. Could it be she had more extra-sensory perception than I realized? A purely self-centered thought entered my head. Was a big, noteworthy scandal brewing in town? I tamped down the selfish moment. Raine was unhappy. It was no time for me to feel giddy about an impending news story.

I tapped her arm to pull her from her worried thoughts. "Look, I'm sure the women are already shrugging the session off. And whatever happens, if the wedding is called off or the relationship is over, you'll still have nothing to do with it. Lana certainly wouldn't blame you. Your powers are great," I assured her and kept my tone as genuine as a good friend could, "but you only predict the future. You don't cause things to happen."

Raine seemed to be weighing my words, but I wasn't sure if I had her convinced. She took a deep breath. "I didn't even tell them what I really saw in the cards. I softened my interpretation. I told them that things might not go smoothly for the wedding."

"See, so no biggie. That could mean anything. Caterers are late delivering foods. Rain and wind on the day of the ceremony. Mothers-in-law have an argument. Trust me, Brooke and Tory are already on their way to the city to pick out shoes for the dresses. They won't give this a second thought. Now, what you need to pull you from this mood is a Bette Davis, a hot grilled cheese and ham on brioche bread." I stood up with renewed energy. "Let's go have lunch."

I lowered my hand and we had a short impromptu laugh as I yanked her to her feet.

"A Bette Davis does sound good right now." I sensed that she was starting to feel better.

We stepped outside. The warm air and woody fragrance that always lingered in the moist summer atmosphere helped revive her more. We walked out her garden gate and headed to our favorite lunch spot. It seemed she was feeling close to a hundred percent, which gave me the go ahead to ask a question that was probably better left unasked. But then, I was, after all, a pokey, proddy journalist with an insatiable curiosity.

"You said you softened your interpretation. What exactly did you see in the cards?"

She hesitated but only for a second. "The cards showed something terrible was going to happen before the wedding."

"Soo, like a really bad storm? Bride comes down with chicken pox?"

"Nope. Worse. According to the cards, someone is going to die."

CHAPTER 7

*L*ana spun around from the bed of the truck and handed me a large basket that was filled with delicious plums, apricots and some of her home baked white chocolate and macadamia nut cookies. "Oh this is too generous, Lana. I'm only helping you set up a campsite."

"Funny little sister. Put that at the end of the picnic table. That's dessert tonight for the bridal party. If there still is a bridal party. Or a wedding, for that matter." She cast a disapproving scowl at Raine, who was too absorbed in her task piling up kindling in the campfire pit to notice.

"It's not her fault." I lowered my voice to make sure Raine didn't hear. "And frankly, if you'd seen her face today after Brooke and Tory left, you'd be worried too."

Lana motioned for me to follow her to the other side of the truck where we could talk in private. "Don't tell me you are starting to believe in her extra sensory powers. Or did you forget the silly little séance at your house, that, shockingly, produced no ghost?"

"Yes, well." Bite your tongue, Sunni. This is your secret to keep, even from your own sisters.

"Honestly," Lana continued, obviously still upset about the entire fiasco. "I think her own mood or blood sugar or whether or not she had a good night's sleep has more effect on her card reading ability than any psychic sense." She waved her fingers in the air to further emphasize her feelings, proving she was more than a little upset. Like me, while she never took Raine's abilities seriously, she also never ridiculed our friend. "I almost lost a big account because of her *interpretations* of those silly cards."

It seemed Raine had been right about Lana's reaction. My older sister could sometimes step on a nerve. "All right, you made your point with the finger waving and all that." I waved my fingers wildly. For the most part, we were successful, supportive adult siblings and we acted in accordance, but occasionally, we lapsed into our earlier years of sibling rivalry. "Everything is always about your bottom line, your profit, the business. I'm telling you that the expression on Raine's face today led me to believe that she had felt something dark in the tarot cards." I decided not to go into the specifics and mention a death because even Raine couldn't elaborate on that stunning proclamation. All she knew was that the cards were warning of an imminent death. I didn't need to fuel Lana's anger or disbelief with that little explosive nugget of knowledge.

Lana produced one of her familiar harrumphs and waved me away with the basket of goodies. I walked the cookies and fruit over to the picnic table. Tonight was just a precursor, a bridal party only event, before tomorrow's bridal shower. Lana had subcontracted a local adventure tour company to set up tents and picnic tables on a beautiful clearing in the campground. Tall yellow birch trees surrounded the site. The canopy of leaves and branches and a nearby lake cooled the early evening air enough that we had pulled on our sweatshirts. That same ceiling of lush foliage would keep the party guests somewhat shaded from the summer heat during the day. Once the sun went down, the surrounding shrubs and grasses would light up with thousands of fireflies, twinkling like haphazardly hung Christmas tree lights. The whimsical display was always a big draw in the summer months and for good reason. They were nothing short of spectacular. I was sure any shadow Raine's dire prediction had cast would be obliterated by nature's twinkling light show.

Lana carried over a foil covered tray and set it on the table. "It's lasagna from the caterer. Precooked, of course. I just hope my idea to heat it over the campfire works."

I followed the direction of her gaze. Raine was setting up a grill with foldout legs near the campfire pit. "I think if they keep it covered with foil, it won't absorb too much smoke." She shrugged. "The glamping party was Brooke's idea, but there's only so much glam you can infuse into a campsite that has very few luxuries."

"I'm sure it'll be fine. Besides, what's wrong with a bit of hickory flavor in lasagna?"

Car tires crunched the rough hewn road leading up to the campground. A blue truck pulled up to the site. Cindy, the second bridesmaid, was behind the wheel. The back doors opened, and Tory emerged along with two other women. The other bridesmaids, I surmised. The tall, slender woman, who looked as if she spent a lot of time outdoors, must have been the cousin from California Lana had mentioned. She had just arrived in town for the shower. The final bridesmaid was wearing her red hair in two braids, and she was sporting a brand new pair of hiking boots. Lana had mentioned that the fourth bridesmaid had grown up next door to Brooke. She'd been asked to join the wedding party as a favor to Brooke's mother. My sister was always expert at finding out all kinds of unnecessary details about her clients.

Brooke climbed out from the passenger seat still looking glum, but her face brightened when she saw the five nicely constructed tents and the pale blue checkered tablecloths my sister had tacked to the picnic tables. Lana had placed clusters of bright yellow sunflowers in heavy clay vases to brighten the shady campsite. Each tent could sleep up to six people and came with a canvas awning to protect the entrance from rain. The sides each had a zipper window to allow for nice ventilation and star gazing.

"It's wonderful, Lana." Brooke's light voice floated across the clearing. Lana waved back to welcome them and then returned to her task of setting out cooking and eating utensils.

"Hey, Sunni," Raine called, "do you think you could help me find some more kindling? I don't think there's enough yet."

My eyes landed on the lofty pile of twigs and branches Raine had already collected. I was just about to tell her I thought there was plenty when I caught her extremely obvious wink. It seemed my friend needed some private conversation time, and a search for kindling would be the perfect excuse.

I headed across the camp. Raine led me along a small trail into the trees. She stooped down to pick up a few twigs. I did the same.

"I didn't realize we were actually going to collect kindling. I thought you just wanted to talk."

Raine stood with a fist full of thin branches. "I did but I needed to make my request look legitimate. As you might have noticed, I'm not exactly on the top of your sister's buddy list at the moment."

"Oh please. That's just Lana. She doesn't hold a grudge long. Once this event is over and everyone is covered in bug bites and filled to the gills with all the treats Lana has provided, everyone will forget all about those tarot cards." I zipped up my mouth, knowing the second I'd finished I'd said exactly the wrong thing.

Raine spun around and stomped through the trees pretending to be absorbed in her task.

I crunched through the dried forest litter behind her. "I said that wrong. I meant—"

Raine crouched down in a pile of sticks. "You don't need to explain, Sunni. I've met plenty of skeptics in my day. I just thought I'd get more support from my best friend."

I stopped and smiled down at her. "Am I your best friend?"

Her back rounded with a deep breath, then she pushed up to her feet. "You're mine, even if you don't feel that way in return."

I walked over and hugged her as well as I could with fists full of twigs. "Of course I feel the same. It's never a dull day when you're around. You're funny and smart. Besides, I'm not nearly as much of a skeptic as you might think."

She wiggled her nose to lift her glasses higher on her face. "Oh? Has something happened to change your mind?"

If you only knew. I searched for a good answer. "Nothing in particular. It's just the longer I know you, the more it all seems plausible."

Feminine laughter and voices filtered through the trees. I glanced back toward the campsite. Lana was showing the girls their tent accommodations. "Sounds like everyone is having a good time." I turned back to Raine. "How about you? Still getting bad vibes or have they lightened?"

Raine shook her head. "I'm afraid that isn't how it works."

"So you're still getting the sense of impending doom?"

Raine's mouth peeled into a straight line, and she pulled her eyes away. "I don't want to say one way or another. I need this job too much." She stooped down to collect more twigs. I stared down at the top of her dark head. Her non-response made it clear that she was still gravely worried.

CHAPTER 8

*M*y sister had left the bridal party feeling cozy and pleased with their well-appointed campsite and plethora of goodies. The three of us traveled back down to Lana's farm. The sun had dropped completely and a sliver of a moon was making its way across the navy blue sky. We kept the conversation in the cab of Lana's truck far away from the topic of tarot cards or psychic predictions.

Raine and Lana were verbally working out the schedule for the morning. The campsite would need to be restocked with much more food and then there were the knapsack gift bags and treat jars to transport. I was just relieved that any of the earlier angst had dissipated. Raine seemed more relaxed, and once my sister was on a roll talking about an event, she never let negative thoughts or distractions get in the way.

The truck headlights lit the dirt road leading to Lana's barn. We'd decided to pack up Lana's truck so she could just head up the hill in the morning. Two cars were parked in front of the barn.

"Looks like you have company, sis."

"Jeez, I've been so busy, I forgot that the groom and his friends were going to wait in the barn before heading up to the campsite to surprise the women."

The truck light illuminated three men sitting on the benches outside of the barn.

"I still think this is a bad idea," Lana said, sounding a little ominous. "A group of teenage girls might be giddy about having a group of boys show up to surprise them, but I don't think Brooke and her friends are going to be overcome with excitement. Brooke was hoping tonight would help bring peace between Tory and Cindy. And after today—" Lana made a point of looking over at Raine. "They really need that peace."

"The men arriving unexpectedly will definitely put a wrench in that plan," I agreed.

Lana parked the truck.

"Which one is the groom?" I asked before we climbed out. The tallest one of the group walked over to a brand new BMW with his phone, deep in conversation. "Never mind. I'm going to assume that's Jeremy Stockton."

"That's him all right." Lana opened the door and climbed out. Raine and I slid out too. Whatever the phone conversation was about, the groom didn't seem too pleased with the person on the other end. He saw us heading toward the barn and quickly ended his call. He forced a polite smile and walked toward us.

"Hope you don't mind that we ate dinner out here on your benches. We tossed our trash in that can on the side of the barn."

"No problem." Lana had a special, ingratiating and professional tone she used with most clients. Tonight's special tone was edged with a little irritation. She was tired. We all were, and now it seemed she was stuck entertaining the groom and his friends while they waited for just the right time to surprise the women. I was fairly certain no time was right, but it was none of my business.

Raine's either apparently. She scurried past everyone and went inside the barn to get to work. If I didn't know any better I would say that she was trying to avoid any conversation with the groom. It wasn't too far-fetched to think that his weepy, distraught fiancée had called him in a panic after the unpleasantness at Raine's shop. And it wasn't too far-fetched that the groom was less than pleased with Raine. His glower as she walked past confirmed that.

"If you guys don't mind," Lana continued, "I could use your help loading up the truck for tomorrow's party. That way I can send my sister home for the night." She tilted a smile my direction.

"Absolutely." Jeremy was a tall, square-shouldered thirty-something whose very dark eyebrows were shaped at an angle that gave him a sort of permanent scowl. Apparently his family company, Stockton Tools, was doing very well as evidenced by his car and his high end adventure wardrobe, slick looking cargo pants, a brand new, pristine coat and leather hiking boots. It seemed he'd purchased the outfit just for the occasion.

Jeremy's phone rang and he pulled it out. "Tom, Bryan give her a hand. I'll just be a minute." He pushed the phone to his ear, and his polite, gentlemanly tone fell away as he snarled the words 'did you get through' into the phone and walked away.

"If that's all, then I guess I'll see you tomorrow." I hugged Lana. "Tell Raine good-bye. She raced into that barn like something was biting at her heels."

"She's avoiding the groom," Lana muttered.

"I guessed that."

Knowing I'd be out well past dark, I had driven my car to the barn. At the time, Lana had given me a hard time about driving five acres to get to her house, but now I was glad I'd made the decision. I was tired.

As my headlights swept across the front porch, I saw a flicker of movement in the front window. A few months ago, I would have been terrified and reaching for my phone to call my sisters. Instead, I climbed out of the car and went inside.

I could see Edward from the corner of my eye as I hung up my sweatshirt on the hook near the door. "Were you waiting up for me?" I asked and turned around. He was drifting in front of the window, pretending like he was just watching the night landscape.

He turned his dark gaze toward me. Sometimes, in just the right amount of light, like the single lamp I'd left on in the front room, I could almost imagine he was flesh and blood, a dashing, well-dressed member of the gentry waiting to ask me for the next dance. Then he spoke with his usually acerbic wit and the fantasy moment vanished.

"I don't understand this term 'waiting up'. Should I be waiting down?"

"It's just a turn of phrase we use, and I'm far too tired to discuss it."

It was always strange to have him following closely at my heels but only hear the sound of my own footsteps. I headed into the kitchen for a glass of milk before bed.

"You were out terribly late," Edward noted. "Do you think it's wise for a woman to be out at all hours un-chaperoned?"

I glanced at the kitchen clock. "It's nine-thirty."

"Exactly."

"The sun has only been down for two hours. I'd hardly call that all hours of the night, and as for the chaperoned part, that's just so very nineteenth century of you. Women no longer require chaperones. I'm perfectly capable of getting around safely on my own." I filled a glass with milk and headed to the bedroom. I stopped briefly in the doorway of the kitchen and leaned back to smile at him. "But thank you for waiting up. Even if you don't actually sleep. It's nice that you were worried." I shut the door to my bedroom before he could ruin the moment with one of his usual biting retorts.

CHAPTER 9

An early morning blue sky and two eager dogs had coaxed me outside for a hike. The family property ran along the base of some rolling hills, which, in turn, eventually grew and spread into the majestic mountain range. The hills provided a nice, easy hiking path, not too steep and not too hard to navigate. The trailhead was adjacent to the asphalt road that led up to the campsite where I imagined the bridal party and their unexpected guests were just rising from their air mattresses with sore backs and cricks in their necks. Lana had provided every comfort for a respectable, luxury camping trip, but an air mattress on hard ground was still just an air mattress on hard ground.

I would have loved to have been a fly on the wall, or, in this case, a firefly on the tent wall to catch the women's reaction when the men snuck up on them. As I got ready for bed the night before, Lana had texted that she sent them up with a tray of brownies she'd had prepared for the following day. She decided they needed to show up with some kind of peace offering in case Brooke and the girls were irritated by the surprise.

The dogs and I climbed through the two boulders meant to keep motorized vehicles off the hiking trail. Newman ran ahead to find a good stick for a game of fetch, but Redford, who was considerably less adventurous and a great deal less energetic, stuck by my side. As I hiked along, I planned my Saturday. I was determined to get a head start on the bridge article with some good old fashioned research. Then, at some point, I would need to make my way to Emily and Nick's place because I was certain the baby goats would be missing me. (Or maybe it was vice versa.) Either way, a baby goat cuddle was on my to-do list.

Newman returned with what he'd apparently decided was a perfectly aerodynamic stick. I wasn't so sure. It had several tiny sub-branches and a dead leaf still attached. Being the super dog mom that I was, I set to work to make it more streamlined, while my dog fell all over himself waiting for me to throw it. I could almost see Redford's eyes roll in his head about the spectacle.

I trimmed off the extra branches and leaf and tossed the stick. It flew end over end and landed a good twenty feet ahead. Naturally, Newman was there to catch it before it hit the ground. But rather than loop around and bring it back, he froze and lifted his head. His ears followed. A second later, a long deep howl billowed up from Redford. Newman dropped the stick and joined him in the crooning session. I looked quickly around to make sure they weren't howling along with a pack of wolves. My human ears finally caught up to their preternatural hearing. Sirens were whining down below. The sound was echoing off the mountainside.

I moved a few feet higher on the trail to get a view of the town below. Red flashing lights spun wildly around on the tops of several emergency vehicles. The breath caught in my throat as they turned down the road that led to the inn and my sisters' houses. I released the gasp I'd been holding as the ambulance and two police cars raced past the entrance to Emily's farm. Lana was up at the campground setting up for the bridal shower, so I knew they weren't heading toward her farm. They sped past the inn and made the sharp turn that led up to the camping grounds.

I watched from the trail. Grit and dust flew up as the tires on the first police car hit the asphalt. It seemed they were heading up to the campsite. I took a few deep breaths to remind myself that there were plenty of other people up at the campgrounds and that Lana and Raine were undoubtedly fine. But I planned to make sure. The police and ambulance disappeared around the first curve.

"Sorry, boys, I've got to make sure Lana and Raine are all right." Redford was far less disappointed than Newman to be trudging back home already. As we passed through the boulders another car whipped onto the adjacent road. It was easy to recognize Detective Jackson in his detective's car, mostly because there just weren't that many men floating around town, or the country or the world, for that matter, who looked like they'd just stepped out of every woman's romantic daydream. He was wearing dark sunglasses, but I got the sense that his eyes locked on mine as he spotted me coming off the trail. Then he returned his focus to the road ahead and disappeared around the curve.

The three of us ran back to the inn. I was breathing hard as I swept up my keys and phone. After a brief interrogation by my house ghost as to why I had raced into the house with a red face and panting like a *madwoman*, I climbed into my car and headed toward the campground.

My heart was back to a major flurry of palpitations when I reached the campground and found that all the police and emergency activity was centered at the bridal party's campsite. Lana's truck was parked near the site, assuring me she and Raine were still there. I did a quick scan of the other cars and quickly catalogued the ones I'd seen in the last few days. It seemed that the truck Brooke and her bridesmaids arrived in and the groom's nice

BMW were the only other vehicles, which meant none of the bridal shower guests had arrived yet. That really narrowed down the list of people who might be sick or hurt or worse. I tried hard not to let my mind shift back to Raine's dire prediction, but it was impossible. Especially as I came upon a makeshift wall of emergency vehicles. My stomach balled like a knot as my eyes landed on Detective Jackson's car. I was certain Jackson would not be called to the site for an ankle twist or chest pains. He was the department's lead detective. Something serious had happened.

I parked far enough back not to be shooed away by the police. I craned my neck as I walked toward the activity and felt a massive rush of relief when I saw Lana's brunette hair and Raine's colorful headscarf. Even though it seemed something terrible had happened, at least I knew that my sister and friend were safe.

As I neared the tents that had been set up for the party, I caught a glimpse of what seemed to be the entire bridal party, the groom and one of his friends. The night before, at the barn, there had been two friends. Had the third man gotten hurt? The men were doing all they could to console the women. Brooke looked particularly distraught and close to crumpling into a sobbing heap. A few of the officers were standing near the cars, but I couldn't see Detective Jackson. I skirted around the back side of some trees that would get me to the campsite without passing the police officers.

Lana spotted me emerging from the trees. She hurried toward me looking as if she'd been up all night binge watching horror movies. "Sunni, you're here." Raine rushed over to join us, shaking her head in an 'I told you so' manner. Her expression matched.

"I heard the sirens. Did something happen to the second groomsman?" I asked.

Lana's brows knitted together. "The groomsman? No. Bryan left last night. Jeremy and his best man, Tom, stayed the night. After they surprised the women during their campfire, Brooke and her friends were feeling uneasy about staying out in the woods alone so Jeremy and Tom stayed."

"Well-planned," Raine said, wryly as a side note.

"I don't understand." I looked past Lana to the picnic tables where the distraught campers were huddled. This time I took a better count of the women. One was noticeably absent. I turned back to Lana. "The maid of honor? Tory?" I said her name as a question. Lana knew exactly what I was asking.

Lana's rueful nod followed. "Dead."

CHAPTER 10

"How? Where? When?" I tossed one word questions at my sister in an attempt to garner as much information as possible before I figured out a way to get closer to the crime scene.

Lana was a smidgen amused by my deep line of questioning, but she tamped down her smile quickly, remembering it wasn't the time or place for amusement. "Raine and I arrived literally minutes after they discovered her. Apparently Tory wasn't in her tent this morning when everyone woke, so Jeremy and Tom went looking for her. They found her lifeless body on the rocky embankment overlooking the lake."

"So it was an accident? A fall?"

"It seems so."

I looked at Raine. She didn't seem quite so certain.

"Raine? You look unconvinced."

I'd gone instinctively into journalist mode. Raine was the perfect interviewee. She was always happy to say what she thought or give her opinion. Or, at least, most of the time. She seemed to hesitate under the watchful eye of her boss, my sister. I decided I would pull her aside later and get her take on it when Lana wasn't in earshot. For now, I needed to get closer to the activity. If it was murder, I wanted to be at the center of the investigation.

The paramedics were returning their equipment to the ambulance, signaling there would be no attempt at revival or any kind of medical intervention which signaled that the person Detective Jackson was studying on the steep side of the embankment was unquestionably dead.

Tory was curled on her side, almost as if she had just decided to take a nap there on the rough, rocky edge. Her shoulder length brown hair seemed to be matted into a nasty tangle of hair, dirt and a thick substance I was sure was blood. There were several rips on the back of her coat. Her hands, which were stark white and stood out against the gray granite and soil background, were crossed limply at the wrists, again making it look as if she was just curled there for a nap.

For no important reason at all, I noted that Jackson's longish brown hair looked particularly wild and there was dark beard stubble on his chiseled jaw. Had he just been pulled from bed? At this hour? Maybe he'd had a late night out on the town. I pushed the entirely unnecessary thoughts from my head and surveyed the area.

Knowing how these kinds of tragedies normally progressed, I was certain Jackson had already placed the obligatory call to the local coroner. While he waited for them to arrive, he was assessing whether or not he was looking at an accidental death or a homicide.

Detective Jackson had pushed his dark sunglasses up on his head affording me a better read on his thoughts. Although the man was irritatingly hard to read. He must have been very good at poker. He kept his expression composed. His extraordinary looks made it seem as if he was just an actor or model at the center of a photo shoot instead of an investigation. The other officer who had been by his side, a woman I remembered from Alder Stevens' murder case, Officer Reed, a weapons expert, had hiked back up to the campsite, possibly to wait for the coroner or to retrieve an evidence kit. A third officer was now stationed at the table where the other members of the party were sitting, consoling each other and making various phone calls. Lana and Raine were sitting nearby on the open tailgate of Lana's truck. I could only conclude that everyone had been asked to stay for a line of questioning. Another indication that there was more to Tory's death than a fall down a steep, rough incline.

One thing was for certain, I wasn't going to find out any details lingering up top at the campground. Fortunately, I was still wearing my hiking boots. Even their thick, grabby soles were no match for the slippery slope leading down to the body.

The initial few steps took some careful foot placement and calculations and a lot of balance. I managed to get about halfway down before the terrain grew slippery with loose debris and rocks. I managed to dislodge enough small stones to start a mini avalanche.

The small river off pebbles alerted the detective below. Jackson had been crouched near Tory's head. He straightened and crossed his arms over his chest, watching with a droll smile as I finished the difficult trek down the slope. His scrutiny was not helping my technique. Twice, I had to stoop down and brace my hand back against the slope to keep myself from somersaulting head over heels right into the victim or the detective, who seemed both amused and irritated about my bold, clumsy hike down the hill.

"Hey, Bluebird, I'd tell you to swing yourself around and head back up the hill, but something tells me you'd just end up down at the bottom anyhow."

I'd forgotten about his annoying nickname, something I'd earned (ridiculously) by wearing a blue shirt while climbing a tree.

I had been trying to get a scoop for a murder story. I was sure I was completely concealed in the tree, only to discover that leaves had not been the best camouflage for a blue shirt. Apparently, Detective Jackson had no intention of letting me forget the incident.

For the last few feet, I squatted down and slid on my boots as if I was on an invisible skateboard. Putting on the brakes took a little more thought and planning. I skidded right past the detective and the victim and finally noticed a jutting tree root to use as a brake. I stretched my leg out and my foot braced against the root, stopping my downward slide. I used the same root and a fellow root to wedge myself into a solid position and pushed cautiously up from my crouch. The angle of the slope was so sharp I was standing nearly face to face with it. I glanced up to the top of the hill and swayed backward a bit before steadying myself.

"It's not hard to see how she might have slipped and fallen to her death on this treacherous hillside." I decided to pretend that I believed it was just a terrible accident, hoping he'd fill me in on more details.

"There's no story here, Sunni. You just risked your own neck coming down that hill. Besides that, you already know it wasn't an accident."

I shrugged. "Maybe." I was close enough to see the matted, wet clump of hair on her head. "Guess it was head trauma," I noted.

"I forgot you fancy yourself a murder sleuth." Detective Jackson took latex gloves out of his pocket and pulled them onto his large hands.

"I think fancy is an awfully frilly term for the woman who pieced together the puzzle of a convoluted murder just a month ago."

"It wasn't all that convoluted, but you did put the pieces together. I guess I can give you that." The worn knees on his jeans stretched white as he crouched back down near Tory's head.

My stomach made a few unpleasant twists and turns as I watched him carefully part the sticky mat of hair. He spread the hair farther and pressed his fingers along the her exposed scalp. Blood smeared the latex gloves as he continued his search.

"Are you looking for a bullet hole?" He hadn't asked me to leave yet, which I took as a sign that he didn't mind me standing there.

"I was until I found this." He glanced up. I'd forgotten about his unearthly amber eyes. They were quite remarkable, but I was sure he knew that. "Are you going to stand over there? If you really want to solve a murder, you've got to get involved with the nitty gritty stuff." He lifted his hands to show me the blood smeared gloves. I swallowed back the bitter taste of my morning coffee and muffin. He knew darn well what he was doing. He thought he could just scare me off the hillside with the *nitty gritty* stuff.

"You're right, Detective Jackson. Can't very well solve a murder from ten feet away." I took my first step but loathed the idea of leaving my nice secure tree root. I had no choice. I took one careful step and another, occasionally using my hands as two extra feet to climb the unstable slope. "No wonder monkeys haven't joined our strictly bipedal way of life. Much easier on all four."

I reached Tory's body. From ten feet away, it was a woman lying still on a hill, possibly deep in sleep, but as I neared, it struck me how utterly lifeless she was. There was nothing, not a twitch of a finger or a movement of shoulder or foot that let you know she had been a living, breathing individual. It took me a second to collect and steel myself for what he was about to show me. The last thing I wanted to do was prove to him I couldn't handle investigating a murder by throwing up at the crime scene.

"If you're going to toss your breakfast," Jackson interjected as if he'd been reading my thoughts, "turn your head that way. Away from the evidence area and away from my boots."

I held my breath, deciding that might help keep me from feeling sick. Detective Jackson spread the hair to reveal a deep, circular dent in the skull. I found that if I focused just on the skull and pushed aside the fact that the skull belonged to a dead woman, a woman I'd just recently seen alive and well, it kept me from feeling nauseous.

I looked up at him. "Someone struck her in the head. Something with a round end. A walking stick?" I asked.

He took his hands away from Tory's hair. He pulled an evidence bag from his pocket and carefully removed the gloves and disposed of them in the bag. We both pushed to our feet. The angle of the slope, the crouched position and the sight of a ghastly skull wound made me sway. Detective Jackson's long fingers wrapped around my arm to steady me. I stared down at his hand for a second. It was big and his grip was strong.

"Going to stay on two feet, Bluebird? I don't want to have to chase you down that hillside."

"I'm fine."

He released my arm, but I could still feel his firm grip, even after his fingers were gone. A few seconds of awkward silence followed, which I broke up with a question.

"Could it have been a walking stick? People use them a lot up here."

"No, unless they jammed it at her like a spear, a walking stick would leave a much different mark, a long dent most likely. This looks more like the end of a hammer." He mimicked the use of a hammer and he was right. Naturally.

"Ironic," I muttered to myself.

"How's that?"

"It's nothing. It's just that my sister mentioned that Tory was a salesperson for Stockton Tools. So death by a hammer seems like a bit of dark irony."

"I saw Jeremy Stockton up at the campsite. He's the one who called in the accident." Jackson walked back around to the front of the body. "How is your sister involved with them?"

"She's not," I said probably far more abruptly than I needed to. "I mean not really. My sister plans events and parties. She set up the camping trip for the bridal shower." I was talking fast, like I was giving some kind of confession. I stopped and took a deep breath. "There were definitely some strained relationships between the bridesmaids. You should probably start with them for questioning."

His dark brow was perfectly smooth as it arched high over his pale eyes. "Thanks for the advice. But I think I'll be able to handle this from here."

"Hey, Jax," Officer Reed called down from above. "Coroner's here."

He waved to acknowledge he'd heard her, then turned back to me. "You should probably—" He paused and reached for something on the front of Tory's coat. He pulled free a twig with flat, waxy leaves.

We both instinctively looked around the hillside for a matching shrub but the steep, gritty slope lacked much plant life.

Detective Jackson held the twig up to get a better look at it.

"Privet," I said quickly. "There's some growing up near the campsite. I saw it yesterday when I was helping Raine gather kindling. That privet shrub is a good ten feet back from this embankment. Maybe someone killed her up there and then sent her down the hill to make it look like an accident. Only they didn't realize the hammer print on her skull would give it away."

Detective Jackson pulled out a baggie and put the twig inside of it. "You do good detective work . . . for a journalist."

"Thanks. I think." We both started the precarious, arduous hike back up the slope.

CHAPTER 11

I'd finished my snooping about and had no choice but to vacate the area when the coroner and his crew arrived. Jeremy was talking rather harshly to a young officer as I walked past the bench where the others had grouped together for comfort.

"I need to get my fiancée home. I don't understand the delay." Jeremy spoke in an entitled, arrogant tone that didn't seem to have much sway with the officer. In fact, probably the opposite. The officer, a young twenty-something guy who looked more than pleased to be wearing a badge, seemed to bristle at Jeremy's almost condescending tone.

"Mr. Stockton," he replied through a tight jaw and then seemed to collect himself. "I understand your concern. I assure you, Detective Jackson will be speaking with you shortly. But until that time, I need all of you to stay on the site."

Brooke looked miserable and pale, like a wilted flower, compared to the day before. Cindy and Kyla sat on either side of her on the picnic bench. Cindy was holding her hand. I couldn't help but notice that her mouth was tilted up and her expressive brown eyes looked shiny with the morning sunlight. Cindy and Tory were apparent enemies but her serene demeanor was not appropriate for the situation. Trina, the cousin from California, looked more than a little miffed that she had just spent good money on a plane flight across the country to sit on a picnic bench and wait to be questioned by police. However, her face did brighten as the young officer pointed out Detective Jackson, who was standing with his impossibly broad shoulders and movie star profile fifty yards away from the picnic tables.

Lana had backed her truck up to the campsite to easily unpack the party goodies, goodies that were no longer needed. I noticed that she and Raine were now sitting in the cab of the truck waiting for the police to give them the go ahead to pack things up. Jackson's team was still searching around for a possible weapon, a hammer or some type of heavy object with a round end. It seemed like a daunting task considering the amount of brush and rugged landscape. Then, of course, there was the body of water below the hillside. I'd heard the words 'dredging the lake' being tossed about.

I walked up to the passenger window and looked inside. Raine and Lana were secretly snacking on the tea sandwiches they had whipped up for the shower lunch. They both stopped chewing and stared at me through the glass with wide eyes and cheeks stuffed like hamsters.

Raine opened the door and I climbed inside. The cab was steamy warm and filled with the aroma of herbal cream cheese and onions.

"I know this looks bad." Lana swallowed and handed me a tea sandwich that was topped with a pretty radish curl. She had gone through a lot of trouble to make sure the shower was lovely. Now, it was never going to happen. "We didn't want all this food to go to waste."

Raine licked cream cheese off her fingertip. "And we were hungry."

I enjoyed my tiny sandwich as Lana handed me an icy bottle of lemonade. She had tied blue polka dot ribbon on the bottles for the festivities.

"I just thought of something." I opened the bottle. "A large group of shower guests are going to be driving up that road soon."

"Cindy sent a group text to everyone letting them know the camping party was cancelled. Without letting them know why," Lana amended before I could ask.

I sipped the lemonade. Lana even knew the best bottled lemonade to buy. Or maybe the cute ribbon just made it taste better. "Probably not the kind of thing to send in a group text."

Lana nibbled another sandwich and handed me one with my favorite topping, pickle chips. "Raine and I noticed you spent a good deal of time down the hill with—with Mr. Dreamy Detective."

"For your information, I was trying to gather evidence about what might have happened to the maid of honor. I think a bridal shower murder might make a good headline."

Lana turned slightly in the seat to look at me. "You are more than slightly warped, little sister."

"Hey, a story is a story, and a gritty, scandalous story sells newspapers." I turned to Raine, who was unusually quiet. She was still snacking on sandwiches but that didn't seem to be the reason for her silence. I'd seen my friend talk right through a slice of pizza and barely take a breath between words or bites. Especially when she had something to say. Which didn't seem to be the case at that moment.

"What's going on, Raine? Did the cream cheese glue your mouth shut?"

Raine swallowed another bite and smiled tightly. "Nope, just don't have much to say."

"Oh just tell her, Raine," Lana said.

"I don't want to discuss the fact that I was right and that all my skeptical friends, who like to secretly roll eyes about my abilities— and yes, I mean the two friends sitting in the cab of this truck snacking on tea-wiches, haven't said a word."

"Well, as long as you don't want to discuss it." Lana elbowed me discretely.

"No one believed me when I predicted something terrible." Apparently, Raine had finished *not* discussing it. "Actually, I did more than that." Raine looked plainly at me. "Sunni, why don't you tell your highly skeptical sister exactly what I interpreted from the tarot cards."

I turned to Lana, who seemed just a touch too amused for the situation. Especially with a murder investigation going on just five hundred feet from the bed of the truck.

"Raine did tell me that she thought the wedding was doomed and that someone would die. We need to take her more seriously." I turned to Raine. "I'm sorry, Raine. Your predictions are coming true, so I won't scoff at your abilities anymore."

Raine straightened in her seat. "That's one Taylor sister apology. But I guess I can hold my breath for the second one."

"Sunni's right, Raine. We need to appreciate your abilities more. I'm sorry," Lana said. "And I'm equally sorry that it looks like I just lost a big wedding account."

"Not necessarily," I said. "When is the wedding?"

"Two months. And it was a big one too. I'll have to cancel the caterers and the florist and the doves and horse and carriage."

I picked up another sandwich from the silver tray. "There were doves and a horse and carriage? Actually, yeah, the bride looks like a horse and carriage type. Sad as it is, I'm sure the maid of honor's death won't keep them from getting married. Maybe they'll just postpone it a month or two. You mentioned that Tory worked for Stockton Tools."

Raine chimed in. "Before I opened up the Pandora's Box of trouble with my tarot card interpretation, Tory was bragging to me that she'd just bought a Jaguar and that she was now top sales-person at the company. She was always kind of a braggart in high school." She covered her mouth to stop a gasp. "Gosh, that was horrible considering she's lying out there dead and cold on the hillside."

"That reminds me," Lana interrupted Raine's moment of contri-tion. "While you were out on the slope with the breathtaking Detective Jackson, did you find out how Tory died? Did she fall or was Raine's intuition right that something sinister happened last night at this campsite?"

"I'm afraid the latter." I looked at both of them. "And it seems the murderer might very well be sitting at the picnic bench behind the truck."

CHAPTER 12

J watched with keen interest as Detective Jackson interviewed Tom Clayborn, the best man. Lana mentioned in passing that Tom worked for Stockton Tools too, a salesperson just like Tory. Tom seemed to do a lot of shifting from foot to foot. He scratched his scraggly beard more than once. It was hard to know if he was nervous about the questions or if he was just not used to being questioned by a detective. And Detective Jackson was an exceptionally tall, somewhat intimidating man with his expansive shoulder width and big arms.

Jeremy was sitting on a rock near the campsite looking grumpy about spending his day on the mountain. The women were sitting on the bench waiting to be interviewed by Officer Reed. They all looked like crumpled flowers, who had been out in the elements too long. Brooke's nose was as red as a tomato from crying, and Trina looked as if she wished she were back in California. Kyla, the fourth bridesmaid still had her hair plaited in two braids. She toyed with one while she answered Officer Reed's questions. She looked only a touch less bored and put out than Cousin Trina.

Raine had walked closer to the road for better phone reception. Lana asked her to call the adventure company about pulling down the tents a day early. I could see her bright blue head scarf through the trees.

Lana dropped a box of plates and cups into my unsuspecting arms, and I nearly dropped them. "If you're going to use helping me pack up as an excuse to watch the shiny coin of a detective at work, then at least make it look good and put some things in the truck."

I followed her with my load to the truck. "I am helping. And for your information, I wasn't watching the shiny coin. Well, in a way I was, but the fact that he's a nice, shiny object has nothing to do with my interest. I was just noticing how agitated the best man seems about the line of questions. I'm certain at this point in the investigation, Jackson is just trying to get a handle on exactly where everyone was last night and if anyone saw Tory leave her tent."

I followed Lana back to the picnic tables. She tossed me a plastic box. "Collect up all the condiments and napkins please."

I swept up the condiments and salt and pepper shakers. Lana had thought of everything. If not for a murder, it would have been a nice, organized bridal shower.

I followed Lana back to the truck. "Lana, you mentioned Raine and you arrived just after they'd discovered Tory on the embankment. I was hiking with the dogs and we heard the sirens. When I saw they were heading up to the campground, I rushed home to get my car. I was worried about you and Raine. What was the scene like when you got here?" Here I was waiting to get some details from Detective Jackson, who was undoubtedly not going to be very forthcoming about them, when I could probably gleam plenty of information from my sister.

"Just like you'd expect when a group of people have discovered that a friend has fallen to her death. Pure chaos and sobbing and a lot of anxious pacing. I did notice one strange thing though. Something that didn't fit in with the rest of the scene."

"What's that?"

"Raine and I climbed out of the truck, confused and stunned by what we saw at the campsite. We didn't know what the frantic, scared faces were about. I thought possibly a black bear had wandered through the camp. None of the campers seemed like the outdoor type, and a bear could easily kick up a frenzy among city slickers. Tom Clayborn seemed to the only person who could put together coherent sentences to let us know what had happened and that the emergency services had been called. As he spoke to me, past his shoulder, I spotted Cindy shuffling out from the copse of trees behind the tents. She looked as dazed and confused as Raine and I felt when we arrived on the scene. And she was pale white, as if she truly had come face to face with a black bear. She was blotting her mouth with one of the blue party napkins. From the greenish pallor of the skin around her mouth and the dark rings around her eyes, I concluded that she had been off in the forest throwing up. Might have been too many treats and champagne the night before. It took a few long minutes before anyone in the party noticed that she had just emerged from the forest looking about as sick as anyone can look while still standing upright. It was Jeremy who caught sight of her first. At the time, I didn't think much about it, but later, it dawned on me just how quickly he left Brooke's side to make sure Cindy was all right. He gently led her to a bench to sit before crouching down in front of her to tell her the news."

"How did she seem to take the news?"

I sensed that Lana considered it a strange question. She twisted her mouth side to side in thought. "I suppose she took it like anyone would, shock and disbelief. She even pressed the napkin back against her mouth as if she might get sick again. Jeremy patted her arm to comfort her, while his bride-to-be stood fifty feet away in near hysterics."

Another short round of sobs pulled us from our conversation. The coroner van's tires crunched over dirt and gravel as it made its slow procession through the campsite. It seemed the police were focused on the privet shrubs directly above the place where Tory's body was discovered.

Lana nudged me. "Here comes you-know-who."

"Who?" I spun around. Detective Jackson's black sunglasses were jammed on the top of his head making his thick head of hair look extra wild. That, coupled with his amber eyes and the long confident strides, made him look slightly dangerous. But his faint smile capped off that assessment instantly.

"I guess I'll collect up the rest of the stuff myself." Lana winked at me as she slipped past.

"Thought you'd be interested to know that your theory of the victim being killed near the privet shrubs and then rolled down the hill is panning out. We collected blood samples from the shrubs and in the dirt leading down to the body."

I held back a grin. "Oh really? Good for me, I guess. Although, something tells me you had already come to that conclusion in your whirling detective brain before I stated it out loud."

The afternoon sun had moved high enough in the sky for its strong warm rays to shoot through the tree canopy. Jackson pulled his sunglasses down over his eyes. "Maybe but give yourself some credit."

"Trust me. I will. What did the coroner say about the time and cause of death?"

Tiny lines appeared on the side of his mouth. He seemed to be weighing whether or not to tell me.

I cleared my throat. "I did come up with a rather crucial theory about the murder. I think I deserve a little insight. Besides, how else am I going to beat you at solving this case, like with the Alder Stevens case, without important evidence?"

"I solved that one way before you, Bluebird."

"Then we must both have different recollections of that day."

"Obviously. The coroner thinks she died around two in the morning. The dew on her clothes and skin seems to corroborate that. She died from head trauma. Most likely a hammer but we'll know more after the autopsy. Unfortunately, no weapon has shown up. Could be at the bottom of that lake."

Lana joined us. It was the first time I'd seen my sister act coy and even a little flirty in a long time. "Detective Jackson," she said in a voice so unlike her usual my face snapped her direction. "Is it all right if the tent company comes here to take them down?" The extra bat of her eyelashes was so unlike her, I wished that I could have taken a picture to send to Emily.

"Actually, Ms. Taylor, we need to search through those tents still. If they could give us two hours."

"Perfect," she said sweetly. "I'll text Raine. She's talking to them right now." I was certain I saw a little over-exaggerated sway of her hips as she walked away. Again, a picture would have been nice for evidence when I recounted it all to Emily. I was already antici- pating the wild round of guffaws we'd have about it.

"I'll let you finish helping your sister." Detective Jackson went back to his officers, who were still collecting samples of fibers and blood on the hillside.

I hurried over to the truck where Lana was just sending another text to Raine. I waited for her to finish, but I forgot that she was a supreme multi-tasker. "Sure seems like there is a lot more than detective journalist talk between you two," she said without looking up from her phone.

"Really? How would you notice that when you were so busy working on your coquettish smile and voice?" I stuck my pinky at the side of my mouth. "Oh, Detective Jackson," I said in my best imitation of Scarlett O'Hara. "Is it all right if we take down the tents? Or maybe you could help us out with those big strong arms."

"Ah ha." Lana pointed at me. "I never said a word about his big strong arms so that description came right from your head."

I rolled my eyes. "I'll go get the tablecloths." I turned to walk away but looked back over my shoulder. "How did that walk go again?" I asked loudly. "Oh, wait, I've got it." I rocked my hips side to side like a pendulum only to discover that I had an unexpected pair of eyes watching the silly display.

Detective Jackson nodded his approval at me before turning back to his team.

CHAPTER 13

*E*arly morning had shifted to late morning and the group at the campsite grew more frazzled and tired with each passing minute. Detective Jackson and his team had spoken to each of them, and he assured them they would be free to go soon. It seemed he was certain the killer was amongst the group of six people. It made sense. Especially if the murder had happened in the middle of the night. Jackson and his team were checking shoes, which meant they'd found some footprints near the crime site.

Lana had lined up a warm lunch of chicken pot pie and garden salads for the bridal shower guests. It had been far past the forty-eight hour deadline to cancel the catering order, so twenty individual pot pies and salads were being delivered to Lana's house. Being the unstoppable hostess, she got permission from Detective Jackson to dash home and pick up the hot lunch, along with a beautiful vanilla and strawberry buttercream cake. Raine had gone with Lana, but I stayed behind hoping to pick up a few interesting nuggets of information.

Detective Jackson was still busy at the main points of interest, the privet shrubs and the hillside where the body was found. I'd been practicing great self-control by not hovering around the investigation area, but I was dying to find out if they'd found anything significant.

With the body removed and most of the evidence collected, Jackson was down to just a skeleton crew of himself and Officer Norton, the young officer who the groom had spoken gruffly to earlier in the day. Norton's fair skin was getting mottled pink by the summer sun poking through the trees. He seemed thrilled to be working closely with Detective Jackson. His straw colored hair kept slipping back and forth as he nodded enthusiastically at everything Jackson said. The two men were busy measuring the distance from the shrubs to the edge of the hillside when I walked up.

"Thirteen feet," Norton called from his crouched position at the shrubs.

Jackson noticed me standing nearby. He straightened and the tape measure rolled up into its metal container. "I think we've got all we need here, Norton. Walk over and let the group know that we're going to do a quick search in each tent. Remind them all that it's just routine so they don't get instantly defensive. Which they will."

"Right." Officer Norton's hair did its back and forth swish as he nodded fervently along with his response. He set off on his spit-shined black boots but stopped before getting more than two steps. He fidgeted with his belt as he turned to Detective Jackson. "Sir, if they ask, what is it we are looking for? Or should I not tell them?" He straightened his shoulders and his gun holster, reminding me a little of Barney Fife from Mayberry. "Wait, I know the answer to that. You told me to let them know it was just routine."

"Good job. You answered your own question." Detective Jackson was politely patient with the man, which made me think he was slightly less cocky than I previously believed. Officer Norton scurried off toward the group. I didn't envy his task. The earlier looks of sadness and concern had shifted to annoyance at being kept so long at the campsite. I was sure that they'd all feel better once Lana arrived with chicken pot pies.

"Patience and clear instructions," I quipped as I walked toward Jackson. "You would have made a good kindergarten teacher."

A short laugh followed. "I don't think I can remember the words to Little Tea Pot, and I think that's a requirement." While everyone else, me included, had cheeks and noses stained red by the sunlight hovering over the campsite, Detective Jackson's golden skin had grown more tan, making the light strands in his hair look like beachy highlights. He just needed a surfboard under his arm and a pair of swim trunks, and he could've been on the cover of a surfing magazine.

I tucked my hands in my back jean pockets to give a relaxed, hey, what's up kind of vibe. I even added in a casual kick at the grit in front of my foot.

He was typing some notes on his iPad. "What can I do for you, Bluebird?"

"Nothing really. I was just thinking that since I was able to brilliantly untangle the strands of the Alder Stevens' murder, I might be able to do the same with this one. That is, if I had a grasp of some of those strands. You know. To untangle."

"Probably already told you more than I should have."

"You mean all the things I already figured out on my own?"

He glanced up from his tablet. I flashed him a large Cheshire Cat grin.

"You're a regular Sherlock Holmes. I don't have much anyhow. I'm going to go through the tents, then I'm sending them all home."

"So you don't think it was any of them? Maybe some drifter hiking through?"

"Never said that. I just don't have enough to detain anyone." He lowered his iPad. "Unfortunately, the soil around the campground is so tightly packed the footprints near the area are a jumbled mess of nothing. One edge of a print right next to the privet shrubs might prove to be something. We made a plaster cast, but even the plaster cast was disappointing. No tread marks. I'm fairly certain all the blood samples we found will belong to the victim. I'm hoping to find traces of blood on something, anything, when I look through the tents. I think the person who planned this had enough forethought to get rid of any evidence and the weapon."

"So it was premeditated?" I rubbed my hands together. "The plot thickens."

"This is not a novel, Miss Taylor. If it were, the murderer would have left some nice big fat clues around this camp. Then I could solve it with very little effort and save the day and earn the kiss from the pretty girl and have it all tied up nicely in the epilogue."

"Interesting, only I'm fairly sure the kiss from the pretty girl happens in the romance genre and not the murder novel."

"Yeah? Then I might be in the wrong business. Anyhow, that's all I've got for you." He looked past me. "I think that's your sister with the food. That'll at least keep the campers happy for a bit while we finish up."

"Guess I'll go help Lana then. Unless you need some assistance with something else?" I stayed for a second hoping he would find some reason for me to stick around.

"I think we've got it covered, Bluebird. Like I've told you before, leave the murder investigation to the experts."

I saluted him. "Yes, sir, Detective Jackson. I will stay out of your way." I turned back toward the tables where Lana was already distributing lunch. The only guests sitting anxiously and waiting for food were Brooke, Trina and Kyla. There was no sign of Cindy. I could see both Jeremy and Tom standing closer to the road for better phone reception. Each man was engaged in a phone conversation and neither of them looked too pleased about still being trapped in the mountains. Perhaps they should have heeded Lana's warning that sneaking up on the bridal shower wasn't the grandest of ideas. Or just maybe one of the men was responsible for Tory's death. Then, if they hadn't shown up, the tables would be filled with rollicking party-goers eating cake, listening to the maid of honor toast over champagne and giggling about slinky lingerie shower gifts. That thought stopped me a few feet short of the picnic tables. Maybe the reason the men insisted on their surprise visit was because it had all been part of a premeditated murder scheme.

Lana and I met at the table at the same time. She was using a linen towel to hold two chicken pot pies. Each pie had a delicious smelling wisp of steam curling up from the vent holes in the crust.

"Where's Raine?" I asked.

"She had to do a few things at home, but she is going to drive up here soon." Lana drew her gaze around the campground. "I'm hoping we can take these tents down soon. The adventure company should be here in an hour."

"I think they are wrapping up shortly."

Brooke and her cousin helped themselves to the first two pot pies that Lana placed on the table. Murder or not, the two women had appetites. Even though Brooke had that slightly emaciated look about her, she dove full fork into the crust.

Lana looked around as she placed one pie she was holding in front of Kyla. She looked excited to have something to do other than sit around and wait.

"Where is Cindy?" Lana asked.

It was an easy and innocent enough question, but it sent an eye roll around the table. "She's off in the woods or at the portables again doing heaven knows what," Brooke said with another eye roll. "She's been disappearing into the trees every hour or so today and last night too. Frankly, I don't know what's wrong with her.

She's acting very strange." She followed up that rather accusatory statement with a large bite of pie.

Lana motioned toward the pie. "Do you want one, Sunni? I brought extra, thinking the police officers might be hungry, but I see we're down to just Detective Jackson and his young, skittish partner."

"I think I'll wait. I told Emily I'd drop by to see her this afternoon. I think she was baking some treats."

"Ah, I see. And would a certain pair of goats be the other reason for the visit?"

My sister knew me too well. "They might have played a part in the decision."

I decided to get a bit more out of Brooke. It seemed now that the shock of the murder had passed and she had some sustenance in front of her, she was ready to talk. And it seemed the topic of Cindy was a sore one. I hadn't expected it, coming from the woman who'd planned an entire night of camping just so her bridesmaids could bond.

I sat down across from Brooke. "Why do you think she's acting strange?" I waited to see if my journalistic straightforward approach would put her off, but she huffed as if she was ready to unload. But not without first making sure Cindy hadn't re-merged from the shadows. It seemed the coast was clear for a rant.

"She's not normally so distant or secretive for that matter. She left the tent three times last night. She claimed she was going to the bathroom twice and to get a drink of water the third time. It kept waking me up. I'd agreed to bunk with her last night because she was nervous about sleeping outside. Jeremy and Tom stayed in one tent and Tory, Kyla and Trina each had their own. Being the bride, I should have had my own, but I wanted Cindy to be happy and comfortable," said the woman who was subsequently throwing her comfortable, happy bridesmaid under the proverbial bus, all while she was out of earshot. Another huff as she dug her fork into the pot pie. "Then she kept me awake all night with her revolving tent door." She was pleased with her choice of words.

"I noticed this morning that she looked as if she wasn't feeling too well," I remarked. "Maybe she is just not the outdoorsy type."

"Mmm hmm," Brooke agreed over a mouthful of food.

I used the momentary lapse in conversation to glance at the other two women. Trina just looked pleased to not have to be part of the conversation. Being an out of state cousin, it was more than possible that she knew nothing about the dynamics between her cousin Brooke and the other girls. And Kyla, who was exceptionally reserved, was far too involved in her pot pie to even listen in.

Lana spotted Jeremy and Tom walking back together toward the tables, and hostess extraordinaire that she was, even in the middle of the wilderness on the fringes of a murder investigation, she hurried to her truck to retrieve two more pot pies from her insulated food case.

Brooke noticed the men approaching and leaned in to add a few more layers to her diatribe. "Frankly, I don't think Cindy ever got over Tory stealing her prom date in high school. She always harbored a good deal of anger about that." Brooke shrugged. "It was just a silly high school boy. Then, of course, after I chose Tory for my maid of honor instead of Cindy—" She lowered her voice, even though no one else on the bench seemed to care to hear what she had to say. "I mean what was I supposed to do, pick two maids of honor?"

"I suppose that would be hard if you had two best friends," I said.

The men arrived at the table, and I got up to give them room to sit with their lunches.

I looked back at Brooke as I headed over to Lana's truck. She focused again on her pie and had no words or smile for Jeremy. I'd even go so far as to call it a cold reception. Brooke, who had seemed like a rather fragile bride-to-be determined to make sure everyone got along nicely, had certainly turned against her good friend Cindy. If I didn't know any better (and I didn't) it almost seemed as if she chose Tory as maid of honor just to upset Cindy. Now the question was, had the high school boyfriend issue and the maid of honor snub been enough to drive Cindy Hargrove to murder? Brooke sure seemed to be implying it.

CHAPTER 14

*R*aine pulled her car up next to Lana's truck while the group was finishing the pot pies. Jeremy and Tom had downed their lunches quickly. They were both too antsy to sit still for long, and Jeremy seemed to have an endless run of phone calls. Unfortunately, the trees and surrounding mountains made cell reception sketchy and each time his phone rang he had to trudge quickly back to the road to talk. It seemed fairly plausible that an important member of a vast tool empire might receive a lot of calls, even on the weekend. Then there was the obvious issue to deal with that one of the company's employees had been murdered. From his expression and tone each time he lumbered back to the road, it seemed he was dealing with a lot of problems which were compounded by the morning's tragedy. Either way, I was certain Jeremy Stockton wanted to kick himself for barging in on the girls' camping trip. If he'd heeded Lana's advice and not carried through with his little surprise, he'd be somewhere else right now, far away from the campgrounds and the shoddy cell phone reception.

My sister was going to take a big loss for this event. Lana had generously offered to refund half the weekend's cost to Brooke, which she gladly accepted. Lana was a clever business woman. I knew she was thinking ahead to the wedding, the big money event. Even though none of this was Lana's fault, without the refund, Brooke might very well have cancelled her wedding plans and taken her business elsewhere. With the refund offer in place, Lana felt free to pass out the food to whoever she wanted. No one could blame Detective Jackson and Officer Norton for taking a brief break from the investigation to indulge in the chicken pot pies. Not that Brooke would have refused a lunch for Detective Jackson, the only person at the campsite who actually looked better as the day progressed instead of drained, weary and red cheeked from sun and wind like the rest of us. Something told me the detective rarely heard the word *no* from women. Although it probably would do him some good to feel the sting of rejection every once in awhile. It might take his cockiness level down a few notches. And I had no idea why I'd let my mind branch off into that particular tangent. I must have been more tired than I realized.

Lana made two trips to Jackson's table to make sure he had everything he needed to enjoy the lunch. She smiled proudly at his fondness for the food as if she had cooked it with her bare hands. After catching me watching her hover admiringly around the table, Lana quickly brushed her hands together as if she'd completed an important task and walked briskly back to her truck.

It seemed that everything was progressing quietly toward an ending when Cindy appeared from the tent looking pale and sickly. Brooke thought she'd gone off into the woods or to the portable restrooms, but it seemed all this time she'd been inside one of the tents. And from the rumpled t-shirt and hair, it seemed she'd been napping. The tents were far enough from the picnic tables that I doubted Cindy could have overheard any of Brooke's earlier remarks, but Cindy definitely looked miserable. Of course, that made sense, considering the circumstances.

Lana handed Raine a pot pie. "Take this over to Cindy please. She hasn't eaten yet." Lana did a double take. "She still looks sick. I wonder if on top of everything else we've all been exposed to the flu on this terrible, epically bad morning. See if she's hungry."

Raine walked away with the pie.

"What can I do to help?" I asked. "I'm starting to fidget with nothing to keep me occupied."

"There's not much to do except wait for the tents to come down."

"You! This is your fault!" The high pitched, frazzled cry sent the birds who were waiting for lunch crumbs from the trees. Cindy's feet plodded weakly in front of her as if her shoes were filled with sand. Her long white finger was trembling as she pointed rudely at Raine. Her distressed, shrill voice caught everyone's attention.

Raine's mouth dropped and her eyes rounded with confusion. She stepped back with the pot pie as Cindy moved toward her. Detective Jackson and Officer Norton had disappeared inside a tent but stepped right back out to see what the commotion was about.

"What on earth?" Lana muttered.

"You knew Tory was going to die. You said as much yesterday inside that squalid, smoke filled creepy house of yours." Cindy's harsh laugh was completely out of step with the rest of her moment of drama. "You call yourself a psychic, but it's a bunch of mumbo jumbo. How did you know there would be a death?"

"That's it," Lana and I said simultaneously. We both rushed to Raine's side.

I put up my hands to stop Cindy's progress. "You're obviously not feeling well." I glanced around to see if anyone from her group of friends would come to help her. She looked terrible and close to getting sick again. Brooke stood nearby with her bridesmaids looking dumbstruck and frozen to the spot. They also didn't seem the least bit inclined to step in and help.

Detective Jackson seemed to be assessing the moment from an investigator's perspective, waiting to see if something significant emerged from the exchange. Lana wasn't having any of it. Raine was close to crumbling into sobs. Lana took hold of her arm and led her to the truck.

I was left standing in front of a highly distraught Cindy. She looked close enough to throwing up that I backed up a few steps to move my hiking boots to safety.

"Let me get you some water," I suggested.

"No." Her pointing finger came out again, but this time it was aimed at me. "I know it was Raine. It had to be. She knew Tory would die."

A tall figure rushed through the trees from the road. Jeremy's face was smooth with worry as he reached the tents. He stuck his phone in his pocket and came to Cindy's side. He took hold of her hand and gently braced her elbow with the other hand as he walked her to one of the tables at the far end of the camp. He was speaking quietly to her, and it seemed to calm her down. Naturally, my gaze shot to Brooke expecting to see a proud bride-to-be, beaming that her future husband was a kind and true gentleman. But I'd been dead wrong with my prediction. Brooke scowled coldly at the pair as they walked away from the camp. It was not at all the reaction I'd expected, but then I also hadn't anticipated Brooke's harsh words about Cindy over chicken pot pie.

I headed toward the truck to catch up to Lana and Raine but was slowed by Detective Jackson who had swept up next to me.

"Care to fill me in on what just happened back there?" he asked.

I cast a sideways glance his way. "I see. You want me involved with your investigation only when I can supply you with pertinent information."

"Yeah. Pretty much. In fact, that's usually how it works. Someone has information I need, and I ask them for it."

I stopped and looked back toward the truck. Raine saw me talking to Jackson. It made her face twist up more in worry. "As you know, Raine is a psychic. She reads tarot cards for people."

He pushed away a fleeting smile and his tongue ran around the inside of his cheek. "Yeah, I know all about her magical abilities."

"See, you're being facetious but you should probably dim that flashy white grin. The bridal party showed up at Raine's on Friday for a card reading. I reached the shop just as the three women, Brooke, Cindy and Tory, your murder victim, were leaving. They were, for lack of a better word, distressed. Raine told me later that the cards had shown her that something terrible was going to mar the wedding. She held back from the women that the cards actually predicted someone would die." I put my hands on my hips. "So what do you think of that?"

"I think I should talk to Raine and find out how on earth she knew someone was going to die."

I grabbed his arm as he turned. He looked down at my grasp. My cheeks warmed as I pulled my hand away. "Wait. No. Raine had nothing to do with Tory's death. You know that as well as me." I took a deep breath to straighten out my words before I stepped into a mud hole again. "I told you that to let you know that maybe we should take Raine's abilities more seriously."

"Right. So, I'm supposed to believe that Raine knew about the murder because the cards revealed it to her?"

"Yes," I said simply and then looked for more to bolster my defense. If only I could reveal my gigantic, enormous, impossible to believe secret. It would make even the world's biggest skeptic a believer. "Look, I'm just saying that I saw her face yesterday and she was upset. She had sensed something when she talked to Brooke and her friends. I've rarely ever seen her so agitated. Maybe it wasn't the cards. Maybe it was just good old woman's intuition." Before he could counter, I pointed at him. "Which exists. Just ask my mom. She always knew when I was lying."

"That's not intuition, Bluebird," he drawled. "That just means you're bad at lying." My fretful expression made him pause. He leaned a little closer to lower his voice. I noticed, (unnecessarily) that there were flecks of cocoa brown in his amber eyes. "Look, I know Raine had nothing to do with the murder, Sunni. But after that accusation, I wouldn't be doing my job if I didn't follow up. I'm just going to talk to Raine. I promise I won't be dragging her away in handcuffs."

CHAPTER 15

*D*etective Jackson had walked Raine to a quiet place at the far end of the camp to ask her some questions. For the first few minutes of the conversation, she was fidgeting with the zipper on her sweatshirt. She adjusted her bright headscarf a million times while she tapped out an entire dance with her nervous feet. But then Jackson placed his hand against her arm. He seemed to be assuring her it was all just routine because she relaxed enough to leave her feet solidly on the ground. Although she was still fiddling absently with the zipper pull.

Lana walked up next to me. She'd been watching the exchange too. "I guess that man knows how to calm frazzled nerves. One touch and a few quiet words, and I thought Raine might melt into a puddle of butter at his feet. I'm going to walk out to the road to wait for the tent people. They should be here any minute. The baby-faced officer is taking his sweet time going through each tent. He still has two more to go before he even gets to the one that Tory slept in."

I looked back toward the tents. "So the fourth one from the end was Tory's?" I decided to switch to investigative reporter mode. Jeremy and Tom were sitting along the embankment talking. Brooke and her friends, growing more anxious to leave the site, had gone for a short walk. It was probably my only chance to gather some possible clues into Tory's murder.

I took a stealthy glance around the camp and saw I was virtually alone. Officer Norton was two tents over from Tory's so I had a few minutes. The tent flap was unzipped which made sense since Tory had left and never returned. I slipped inside. A plush, downy sleeping bag that looked brand new as if she had purchased it for the trip laid unzipped like the tent flap. Tory had even brought along a plump down pillow for her *roughing it in the wild* weekend. A Louis Vuitton handbag sat next to the pillow, and an open suitcase sat alongside the sleeping bag. The bag was filled with designer sweaters and jeans. Even her socks looked expensive. Tory had money, or at the very least, she liked to spend it. It seemed I wasn't going to find much on my clandestine tent excursion, but as I turned I kicked something. A cell phone slid out from the edge of the sleeping bag.

I remembered a napkin I'd stuck inside my pocket after helping with the lunch. I pulled it out. I listened for the sound of footsteps outside of the tent, but they would be hard to hear over the sound of my own racing heartbeat. I hadn't done anything quite so sneaky in a long while.

I wouldn't have time to gleam much information from her phone, but I used my own phone to get a picture of a recent text conversation with Brooke. I tapped over to her contact list and quickly brought up another text conversation with, of all people, Cindy. I snapped another picture. Someone Tory had given the illustrious title of 'Jerkface' was next on the list. I clicked a picture of Tory's conversation with 'Jerkface', concluding it was possibly someone she disliked.

My thumb accidently swept the screen and opened the app for

jotting down daily reminders. I could hear Detective Jackson's deep voice. He must have ended his conversation with Raine and he'd joined Officer Norton on the tent search. I took a quick picture of some of Tory's reminders and quickly replaced the phone under the edge of the sleeping bag.

Light and fresh air poured into the tent. My face popped up. Detective Jackson looked less than pleased to see me.

"Ha! I took care of that little scoundrel," I said confidently. "I saw a squirrel dash inside the tent, and I wanted to make sure the rascal didn't disturb anything."

Jackson looked pointedly at the crumpled napkin in my hand.

"Yes, this is a napkin, here in my hand." I held it up to verify that fact. "I thought I might have to grab the lil' sucker by his big, fluffy tail, but he took one look at the scary woman with the napkin and hightailed it out of here." I added a fake laugh. I wasn't sure how to take his silence, especially coupled, as it was, with a somewhat stony expression, an expression that really worked with the unbelievable symmetry of his face. There I was again on a descriptive tangent about the man. "How do you like the way I cycled back to the tail thing?" I laughed again but cut it short after I decided it sounded extra fraught with guilt. I shoved the napkin into my pocket and surveyed the tent once more. "All clear of forest critters and as you can see, nothing was disturbed. So carry on with your detective stuff and just let me know if you need any more help with rogue squirrels." I ducked down to leave the tent.

"What about rogue bluebirds?" he quipped.

I stopped and straightened. "You look like the kind of guy who could handle a little bluebird."

"Yeah? I'm not so sure about that. Or maybe I just stumbled onto an especially wild one." Jackson gazed at me just long enough to unsettle me even more than being caught in the act of snooping through evidence.

His comment wiped away my train of thought and any chance of a decent response. I pointed back over my shoulder. "I'll just get out of your way." I ducked down and scurried from the tent like a squirrel . . . or a bluebird.

CHAPTER 16

*T*he two men sent to dismantle the tents had been given the go ahead to start on the first three. Lana helped everyone carry out their personal items. Raine seemed more inclined to stay away from the entire event. She had settled herself into the cab of the truck where I found her scrolling through emails on her phone.

I climbed in next to her, pleased to get out of the slightly annoying breeze that had been tickling and dancing through the trees since late morning.

"How are you doing?" I asked.

"You mean other than feeling like I've been accused of murder?"

"Raine, no one accused you of murder."

She pushed her black rimmed glasses higher on her nose as she faced me. "Uh, Cindy's exact words were 'this is your fault'. And I'm sure Detective Jackson has a few question marks and stars next to my name on his shiny little detective's iPad."

"You're being silly. And frankly, I just don't think he's the star type. Check marks maybe but little stars, nah?" My attempt to make her smile failed miserably and rightly so. I pushed my shoulder against hers. "He's just doing his job. He knows you didn't kill Tory."

"He's also a major skeptic. He doesn't have to say it. I could just see it in those ridiculous jewel-toned eyes of his." Raine whipped the scarf off her head and combed her dark hair back with her fingers. "Why on earth should a man be blessed with such natural beauty? Seriously, gold topaz eyes fringed by thick black lashes. Not fair."

The stress of the day had gotten to both of us. We laughed in unison as we scooted down in the seat and pressed our knees up against the dashboard to rest for awhile. It had been a long morning and now morning had coasted into afternoon.

Raine pulled at the white threads stretched across the knee hole on her very faded jeans. "I sure didn't expect that dramatic display from Cindy. One minute I'm walking a pot pie over to her and the next she's pointing and accusing me of murder. And the great slice of irony there is that, of all the people at this campsite, I think she's the killer."

"Why do you think that? Other than the high school boyfriend thing. I think there's a statute of limitations on prom date stealing."

"I don't know. It was a pretty big story at the time. Secrets and whispers and tales of Cindy freaking out could be heard from the cafeteria all the way out to those weird round buildings where auto shop was housed. Cindy even skipped out on the grad night party because she was so upset and humiliated. And then what does Brooke do to throw gasoline on the fire?"

"She picks Tory to be maid of honor," I finished for her. "I suppose if Cindy is the type to hold a grudge, then—"

"Which she is as evidenced by her baseless attack on me."

"Yes but that's a contorted definition of grudge. Cindy wasn't harboring hard feelings about your interpretation of the cards. I think she saw you and it reminded her that you predicted something terrible was going to happen."

Raine dropped her knees and sat up. She reached into the glove box and pulled out a stick of gum. "Certainly not a reason to accuse me of murder."

I sat up from my slouch too. "You have to admit, the coincidence is pretty astounding." I knew I'd worded it wrong, but there was no way to retract it.

Raine had to open and shut her mouth in exaggerated movements to get the hard stick of gum under control. But she managed to scold me right over the mouthful of gum. "That's because it's not a coincidence. I saw it in the cards and then it happened. No coincidence. Just a prediction and a pretty darn good one at that."

"You're totally right. Excuse my use of the 'c' word. Let's half switch the topic. Did you happen to notice that Brooke was suddenly very bitter toward Cindy? Brooke went off on quite a tirade about Cindy while she was guzzling the pot pie. She mentioned that Cindy was acting secretive and suspicious, and she added that Cindy had left the tent they were sharing three times."

Raine had the gum softened to an acceptable level. Its fruity fragrance filled the cab. "I hope Brooke mentioned all of that to Detective Jackson."

"I'm sure she did." That was when it dawned on me. "Oh my gosh, of course. That's why Cindy accused you. Brooke no doubt mentioned something about Cindy's peculiar behavior and her secret excursions out of the tent. In turn, Jackson probably asked her about those trips."

Raine slapped her thigh. "Cindy was looking for someone else to put under the murder spotlight. Namely me."

"That's it. Gosh, that does make Cindy look even more guilty, doesn't it?"

"It does." Raine turned to look through the back window of the truck. Looks like they've got half the camp down." She spun back around. "I wonder if Cindy was putting on an act, pretending to be sick for some sympathy or to make herself look less villainous."

"I don't know about that. It's pretty hard to fake nausea. It looked pretty real."

"Ah ha," Raine said again. "That proves it then. She's sick to her stomach because she killed Tory, and she keeps reliving the moment when she smashed Tory in the head."

I moved my head side to side. "Interesting theory but plausible. I guess we should probably get out and help Lana. Then we can all get out of here faster, and she won't be shooting us sour lemon looks the rest of the day."

"Yep, my brief little retreat is over. I know I didn't kill Tory, so I'm just going to brush it all off."

"Good plan."

We climbed out of the truck. As I walked around the open tail-gate, I spotted Brooke's cousin, Trina, standing near the road. She had her duffle bag sitting at her feet, and she looked about as unhappy as a person could look. I hadn't spoken much more than polite niceties to the woman, but I thought it wouldn't hurt to get her take on the entire event. I had no idea if she was willing to talk, but from the grim set of her lips, it seemed as if she was holding in quite a bit of anger. That was probably mostly due to having spent money on a roundtrip ticket from California just to sit at a murder scene all day.

It seemed to me she was waiting for a ride. Maybe she'd gotten tired of the whole thing (who could blame her) and she'd decided to call for a ride down the mountain rather than wait for Brooke and the others.

"Tell Lana I'll be right there," I told Raine. I reached into the ice chest in the back of the truck and pulled out a bottle of water as a nice offering to open a conversation. I was fairly good at reading people, and Trina seemed more the aloof, unfriendly type. But it was worth a shot. She had, after all, been with the bridal party since the beginning of the camping trip. She'd witnessed all the interactions and nuances between the women, even if she was technically the outsider of the bunch.

Trina was probably the only other person, besides the ever golden Detective Jackson, who looked even better after a day outside. She'd arrived looking fresh and tanned, just like one would expect from the west coast, and the harsh summer sun at the high elevations had only enhanced that glow.

Her hazel eyes stood out in her suntanned face. She looked surprised to see me emerge from the trees with a bottle of water.

"I thought you might need this for the trip down the hill."

She gladly accepted the water. "I switched my flight back home. I've got to be at the airport in two hours, so I couldn't wait for Brooke. Once the detective said I was free to go, I pulled up my Uber app and found a driver." She leaned in closer, rather unnecessarily since there were no other ears around. "That is one fine looking detective, by the way. Still, I don't want to sound rude and I love nature and the outdoors, but I can't wait to get out of this darn forest. What a disaster."

I had expected her to be far more tight-lipped, but it was entirely possible that she had badly needed someone to talk to after such a horrible morning. The other women were so into their own emotions and problems, Trina had sort of been left in the cold. The odd man out. Cousins didn't necessarily mean they were close. Especially if they lived on opposite coasts.

"I'm sure you weren't expecting this after a long flight from California." I wanted to keep the conversation going, hoping it could lead into some details about the night before when everything was still heading toward a big bridal shower instead of a murder investigation.

Trina's narrow shoulders bunched up. "I tried every excuse in the book to get out of this trip, but Brooke wouldn't take no for an answer. She was the same way when we were kids. If she didn't get the Barbie with the princess gown, then she refused to play."

"So you two were close growing up?" I had to make sure to hide my journalist's tone. Trina didn't seem to mind the prying questions.

"Only until we were eight. Then my family moved to California, and we only saw each other at Thanksgiving. I agreed to be in the wedding because my mom begged and pleaded with me to say yes. Brooke's mom is her sister. Then I thought, well a camping trip and party might not be too terrible, but wow was I wrong. And not just because of the obvious."

"Yes, it's so tragic. A heartbreaking way to end what was supposed to be a joyous event."

A short puffy sound left her lips. "Joyous. Not sure where the trip was heading, but it was hardly joyous."

I glanced back through the trees. The third tent was down, and it seemed that Detective Jackson was wrapping things up. There was no sign of Trina's ride yet. It seemed I had a few more minutes to squeeze out some more details. It was easy to surmise that things weren't going too smoothly the night before after Brooke's attitude toward Cindy and the tiny little fact that someone had wound up dead.

"Why do you say that? Was there trouble last night? Had Tory argued with someone?"

For the first time, Trina paused and seemed to ponder whether or not she should be talking to me. The moment of disappointment I felt thinking I'd just lost her as a source of information vanished when she shrugged indifferently and continued.

"I don't have much insight into the relationships between my cousin and her friends. Like I said, I moved away at an early age. I've only ever met Jeremy twice before this. My aunt might have bragged just a little too much about him because I was not terribly impressed. He wasn't all that attentive to his future bride, even after the nightmarish discovery this morning. Frankly, he seemed to be more worried about Cindy than his own fiancée." I had witnessed the same thing about Cindy and Jeremy and I wondered if that was the reason for Brooke's cold assessment of her friend at lunch. Before I could ask her to elaborate, she continued on to a different topic.

"All the other bridesmaids were Brooke's longtime friends, especially Cindy and Tory. Frankly, last night it felt like high school all over again," Trina continued. "Kyla basically stayed to herself. I think she was seeing the same shades of high school behavior as me and wanted nothing to do with it. Cindy, Tory and Brooke were being snippy with each other one minute and besties the next. By the time we sat down to have cocoa by the campfire, they were all good friends again. Tory and Cindy were both going out of their way to show Brooke that they were the better friend by showing their enthusiasm for the night out under the stars. Halfway through the campfire, Brooke's demeanor changed and she seemed upset. Then the guys showed up. Jeez, they were about as subtle as a herd of buffalo. We had seen Jeremy's car on the road below and figured out their scheme long before they *surprised* us." She lifted her hands for air quotes.

"That's funny. They were so sure they would scare you girls witless while you sipped your cocoa and told ghost stories. But I guess that plan fell flat. Along with the whole weekend, I suppose."

Trina looked at her phone. She'd gotten a text from the driver. "He's five minutes out. I'll be free of this bad dream soon. Once the guys arrived, things between the three women got strained again. Then there was the weirdest moment of all. Thankfully Brooke didn't see it."

I had less than five minutes and I was going to find out about the weirdest moment of all, even if I had to hitch along with the Uber ride.

We'd connected enough that I sidled up to her like a friend ready to hear some juicy gossip. "Weird how?"

"I decided to get ready for bed, so I hiked along the path to the bathrooms. Cindy had gone a few minutes ahead of me, so I expected to see her. But what I didn't expect was to find her standing in the shadows of the restroom crying. And she wasn't alone." She paused for dramatic effect. "Jeremy was comforting her and not a pat on the back, *there, there* kind of comfort. He had his arms around Cindy, and her face was pressed against him. I snuck into the bathroom so they wouldn't see me. The last thing I wanted was to step into some kind of sticky love triangle."

A car turned the last curve to the campsite. "Phew, there's my ride. Nice talking to you." She grabbed her duffle. "Thanks for the water."

"Have a safe flight home."

CHAPTER 17

I could have stood in the shower for hours, washing away the dust and the sweat and the aggravation of the long morning, which stretched into an equally long afternoon. The moment Detective Jackson released everyone to go home, a cloud of grit kicked up in a frantic storm as the campers peeled away from the site. The rest of the tents came down quickly. Raine and I helped Lana finish up before hopping into our own cars to head home. Apparently, Jackson wasn't exactly thrilled with my covert exploration of Tory's tent. He hardly spoke to me afterward.

I pulled on my shoes. The long shower and a good lunch had given me renewed energy. My original plan was to sit down at the computer and do some research for the bridge article, but after being confined to the campsite most of the day, I felt like being outside. A walk to Emily's farm and a short snuggle with my two favorite 'cartoon characters', Emi's baby goats, were just what I needed.

I swept through the kitchen and grabbed an apple from the

basket on the kitchen table. Newman and Redford were outside in the yard, no doubt harassing a squirrel or rabbit.

I'd left the front window open to air the house out. As I crunched my apple, I heard Edward's posh deep drawl float through the screen.

"That's it my beauty. You like that, don't you?" he cooed softly.

I nearly choked on my bite of apple in my haste to get out to the porch and find out who he was talking to. My heart stomped around in my chest a few more seconds before returning to normal. Edward was at the front edge of the porch, his border wall in this world, feeding an apple to Emily's horse, Butterscotch.

My footsteps on the porch snapped them both out of the apple treat session. Butterscotch's big muzzle kept swishing side to side in rhythm with her long ivory colored tail as she ground the fruit into apple sauce. Bits of it clung to her chin whiskers.

"She's a good horse," Edward noted. "Sturdy build, perfect for pulling a plow. Of course, I prefer a tall-legged horse for hunting and running across the countryside." He said it so matter-of-factly as if he'd forgotten that it didn't matter what type of horse he preferred because he would never ride one again. And as his image wobbled and faded some, I knew that for a brief moment that had been the case. His features sharpened. "Lord, how I miss feeling the wind in my face, the scent of grass so strong I can taste it, my body moving with the horse as we race over the landscape. Nothing can bring a human closer to flight than a good gallop on a fast horse."

"With the exception of actually flying in a plane. And then there are hang gliders and helicopters . . ."

He handed off the last chunk of apple to Butterscotch and turned to face me. "I've seen those strange metal birds in the sky many times. Can you feel the wind in your face on an airplane?"

"If you can, then you're in big, big trouble." I whistled for the dogs. They came bounding out from the back of the house. "Are you guys up for a visit to the farm?" The word *farm* was their cue to head off toward Emily's house. They loved getting there ahead of me to sneak up on the chickens.

I hopped down the steps. "Well, I better walk Miss Butterscotch back home, and I've got some baby goats to visit."

"Goats," Edward scoffed. "Why would anyone require a goat visit? I once took my frock coat off to play a game of lawn tennis at a neighboring estate. By the time the game ended, there was a hole as big as my face in the back of the coat. The goat still had black threads of fabric dangling from its mouth."

"And that's why they are so much fun. What other animal can provide great excitement to a dull game of lawn tennis?"

I clucked my tongue, which was all that was usually needed to coax Butterscotch to follow me. But the mare's big head stayed right where it was, staring over the porch railing like a horse looking over its stable door. I clucked again but louder, making it sound less like a cluck and more like a forced strangled sound. Butterscotch's massive feet stood in place.

I stopped and put my hands on my hips. "She thinks you've got another apple. I think you need to do your 'poof gone from sight thing', otherwise I won't be able to get her back home."

"Poof?"

"Oh boy, here we go again."

"I don't poof. I glide. I vanish. I walk through solids. But I don't poof."

I waved him toward the house. "Then glide and vanish right through that solid wall, so I can get the horse to follow."

Without any more argument, rare for Edward, his image disappeared. Butterscotch's ears shot forward. It seemed she could still sense his presence. She neighed softly toward the house.

"You have to leave the porch altogether," I called into the air. "She knows you're still there, and this explains all those times when the dogs were staring expectantly into an empty room."

I decided to start walking, assuming the horse would catch up once she realized there were no more apples or charming British gentlemen to flatter her in dulcet tones.

My prediction came true. About halfway along the path to Emily and Nick's farm, Butterscotch's wide hooves beat a clippity clop rhythm on the packed dirt behind me. She decided to just keep going and left me with a nice cloud of dust as she continued on to the farm.

The distant sound of agitated clucking assured me my dogs had arrived safely at the farm.

Nick was mending a wire fence at the far end of the chicken yard. Emily and Nick had built colorful, whimsical coops to house their flock of egg layers. Nick pulled his hand from the fence, still holding his wire cutters, and waved.

Once the chickens had been sent into frantic chaos, my dogs quickly lost interest. They loped toward the house and up the back steps. Redford stuck his paw against the back door screen to let Emily know we'd arrived. Both dogs nearly pitched backward off the porch steps when the friendly paw was met with a loud bleat on the opposite side. Cuddlebug's cute muzzle pushed against the screen.

"My babies!" I chirruped as I ran up the steps. Both baby goats were trotting around Emily's kitchen, slip-sliding on the tile floor as they hopped and danced in anticipation of their milk bottles.

"You're just in time, Auntie Sunni." Emily turned around from the sink holding two baby bottles.

The squeaky noises in the kitchen grew so loud, both dogs darted back outside without even waiting for a dog treat.

"I guess I can check goat and sheep herding off their list of possible occupations. Which, considering it's what Border Collies are bred for, leaves them with few options."

I pulled up the squat wooden stool to sit down for the goat feeding. Emily handed me both bottles. By the time I positioned myself, four tiny front hooves rested against my thighs. The goats latched on and pulled and tugged and made the cutest sounds ever as they emptied the bottles.

"I really needed this after the terrible morning."

Emily poured herself a cup of tea and leaned against the kitchen counter to watch. "Lana told me that one of the bridesmaids was murdered. Still can't believe it. What kind of monster would kill someone in the middle of a bridal shower?" She laughed dryly. "I guess the same kind of monster who would kill someone, period. I suppose if you're planning to commit murder you don't really think much about the time or place. What happened exactly? Lana didn't give many details, only that it was a horrendously long morning."

"From the bits and pieces I gathered from Detective Jackson, it happened sometime in the middle of the night after the campers had gone to their respective tents. Tory, the maid of honor and victim, was in her own tent, so no one knows exactly what time she left it. I actually got to stand next to the body while the detective was inspecting it. I was there when he discovered the perfectly round wound on her head indicating that it was homicide and not just a tragic fall down an embankment."

Emily's nose crinkled. "You're brave. I don't think I'd want to get within a hundred feet of a grisly scene like that."

"Then I guess it's a good thing you went into chicken farming instead of investigative journalism."

"Couldn't agree more. Do they have any idea who killed her? It's awful to think someone in the bridal party did it. Lana said there seemed to be some tension between a few of the women."

"It seemed two best friends had been vying for the maid of honor position, and the one who got it ended up dead. There were definitely some bitter feelings floating around the campsite. But I don't think Detective Jackson narrowed anyone down yet. They couldn't find the murder weapon. He said something about searching the small lake at the base of the hillside."

"Sounds like it could be a long investigation."

Tinkerbell and Cuddlebug finished their bottles just seconds apart, but they weren't going to give up on the idea that the bottles would magically refill if they just tugged at the nursing nipples enough.

Emily set down her tea. "Here, let me take those bottles before they destroy yet another set of nipples." She took the bottles from me and I commenced with the snuggling, whether the goats were up for it or not.

"Don't squeeze them too hard," Emily quipped. "They're stuffed full of milk."

"That's right." I released my tight hold on a squirming Cuddlebug for a second, then gave her one more squeeze before letting her trot off with Tinkerbell.

"That's enough house time, girls." Emily shooed them both out the door. "Now that you're done being nursemaid, would you like some hot tea? It's raspberry and lemon."

"Hmm, yes please." I walked to the sink to wash my hands and noticed a plate of chocolate dipped shortbread sitting on the counter. "Is this delicious looking batch of cookies for anyone special? And by special, I mean a loving sister who brought your wayward horse home again."

"It just so happens I made it for my special sister, even before I knew she brought my horse home again." Emily put the kettle back on the stove and carried the cup of tea over. "That Butterscotch. I sometimes think she likes it better at the inn than here on the farm."

I was so deep into the rich deliciousness of the cookie, I wasn't thinking clearly. I just blurted the first thought in my head. "Well, with Edward tossing her chunks of apple from—" I froze mid-sentence. I knew I was wearing a wild-eyed expression, but I couldn't stop myself.

Emily's dark blonde eyebrows knitted together. "Who is Edward?"

"What? Who? No. There's no Edward." I waved my hand and produced a ridiculous fake laugh. "Edward who?" I laughed again and tried hard to make it sound more genuine. I could tell by the still puzzled look on Emily's face it wasn't working. "I don't even know where that name came from. I meant Redford." I took a sip of tea and drank it too fast. "Ouch, hot. Anyway, that's what I meant. Guess I was just up on that mountain too long today. And then with the murdered bodies. I mean body. There was just the one." I held up my finger for a visual of the number one.

Emily nodded like she understood. I breathed a sigh of relief. She went to the stove to turn off the kettle. "So Redford has learned how to toss apples to my horse?" She looked back at me with questioning blue eyes.

"Uh yes, he's quite clever, my boy Redford." I picked up another cookie and shoved it into my mouth. "Tho gud," I mumbled over my mouthful. I was prepared to eat the entire plate if it kept me from opening up my big mouth again.

CHAPTER 18

The sun was long gone and a warm, gentle breeze coasted over the long tips of the grasses surrounding the house. The nearly moonless sky cast a shadowy blanket over the landscape, creating the perfect backdrop for the nightly firefly carnival in the front yard.

I sat on the top step, hugging my knees as I watched the twinkly display of nature's most whimsical exhibit. They were truly astounding little beetles, creating what seemed like a well-choreographed dazzling light show, glittering gold stars that seemed to have fallen from the sky right into the fields surrounding the inn.

Redford scratched at the screen door, signaling he'd had enough of nature. I stood up, brushed the dust from my jeans and headed inside to my computer. The long, strange day had left me with little time for researching my next article, but the long, sleepy summer night would give me the perfect chance to sit down and do a little reading about the Colonial Bridge project.

Emily had sent me home with more of the chocolate dipped

shortbread and a mason jar filled with her homemade berry lemonade. I decided to forgo the cookies for the evening since I'd already eaten an obscene amount, but I poured myself a glass of lemonade. Emily had mashed a delicious mixture of blackberries and raspberries into a simple syrup before dropping the whole glorious concoction into her homemade lemonade. Before I left the farm, I told her to write down the exact directions so I could add the recipe to a box of food ideas I was keeping for the future bed and breakfast. If only the Cider Ridge Inn was ready to open as a true bed and breakfast, then I wouldn't have to spend my Saturday night researching dull bridge building projects.

I set my laptop up in the kitchen and sat down with my lemonade. I'd grown a sort of sixth sense when it came to Edward. I always knew when he was lurking about, even before he revealed himself. I wasn't sure if I would have that same extra sensory perception with any other members of the spirit world or if it was limited to just my particular house guest. I hoped it was the latter. The last thing I needed was to start seeing and talking to all the ghosts I passed in my daily life. Edward Beckett was about all I could handle.

"I know you're looking over my shoulder, so you might as well just appear. No sense in hiding."

"I wasn't hiding. I was just feeling lazy. Didn't feel like making an appearance."

"Lazy? How can someone who doesn't need to eat or sleep and who defies gravity be lazy?"

As I spoke, Edward drifted past me and sat up on the kitchen counter, one of his favorite perches. "What are you doing on that blasted metal box this time?"

"Work. Since I'm not a ghost with free lodging and few living expenses, I need to keep my job. I can't afford to be lazy. And before you correct me, I know you don't have any living expenses. I was just using the phrase to make a point."

"I wasn't going to say a word. I don't even understand the concept of living expenses."

I typed Colonial Bridge and Firefly Junction into the search bar and rested my hands. While I waited for the topic to come up, I launched into one of my daily Edward lessons. "Living expenses are food, shelter, clothing, all the things that keep me from living in a cardboard box on the side of the road."

"Oh, those. I had no living expenses. I was given a monthly allowance to spend how I saw fit. I lived on the family estate and food was provided by a robust cooking staff. Clothing came by way of Irving Young, the family tailor, and transportation arrived at my door whenever I ordered the carriage to swing round."

"Yes but the cooks weren't actually providing the food. They just cooked it and the tailor—you know what, never mind. You obviously lived in a much different time and under much different circumstances. And I've got some research to do." The first few entries were about the bridge's history and a few other boring blog posts. Farther down were some minutes from the Firefly Junction town council. I clicked on the link. Apparently, the Junction Council had met with the city managers of the Birch Highlands and Smithville, the two towns connected to Firefly Junction by the Colonial Bridge. The meeting agenda was a year old. The minutes showed that the three towns had agreed to secure private funds to supplement the city funds for the bridge's upgrade. There was a long engineer's report attached to the minutes. I would eventually open the report, but I was sure it was going to be full of technical jargon that was beyond my knowledge base.

"Have you found what you're looking for?" Edward asked.

"To be honest, I can't answer that because I don't know exactly what it is I'm looking for. Parker, the newspaper editor, gave me an assignment about refurbishing a local bridge, but the more I read, the duller this story sounds."

I clicked on another entry for subsequent minutes that included reference to the Colonial Bridge project.

"I suppose bridges only make interesting stories when they collapse," Edward noted.

I nodded in agreement. "As morose as that sounds, I'm afraid you're right. And from what I can tell, as I read through the town minutes, the only reason for the delay in renovation has been weather and the hired contractor's busy schedule." I slumped back against the seat. "I was hoping there was at least some misused fund scandal or something nefarious behind the delay."

"Perhaps you'll get lucky and the bridge will collapse before your deadline."

"No, I don't want that. Obviously. My gosh your ghostly mind sure has some dark corners in it."

"Well, I am dead. It's not as if I have a string of cheery thoughts running through it."

As I reached up to close the laptop, my eyes drifted down the screen and landed on the words Stockton Tools. According to the minutes, the company was one of the major funders for the project. "Hmm, I wonder," I said to myself.

"Wonder what?"

I closed my laptop. "Just thinking aloud. The murder I was telling you about earlier, the woman who died was working for Stockton Tools. Stockton Tools is funding the bridge project."

"Do you think there's a connection?"

I considered his question. "Maybe not between the murder and the bridge but since I'm working on the bridge article, I have every reason to go to Stockton Tools and ask some questions about the project. And while I'm there, I can find out a little more about the murder victim. I can snoop around to find out what kind of relationships she had with her coworkers." I slapped the table. "That's it. I've been trying to figure out how I can get close to the murder investigation without stepping on Detective Jackson's toes and this is it." After narrating the entire plan, I stood up. "Thanks for that."

"Thanks for what?" Edward drifted over to the brick hearth where Newman and Redford had curled up on their pillows. He ruffled Newman's ear with his transparent fingers and the dog twitched in his sleep.

"Thanks for helping me see a connection. I'm going to use my assignment to uncover evidence to solve Tory's murder."

"You're welcome, I suppose. And who is this Detective Jackson with the oversized toes?"

I laughed as a quick vision of Jackson wearing long clown shoes dashed through my head. "His toes aren't actually oversized. Although, I've never seen him without shoes so anything's possible. Anyhow, he's the lead detective on the murder case. I met him on the last case, where, even without all the perks of working for the police, I managed to solve the murder of the local high school custodian." My momentary metaphorical victory lap was cut short by the somewhat forlorn expression on Edward's face. He was still teasing the dog in his sleep and didn't realize I'd turned to face him. It astounded me how much emotion I could read on a man who was purely vapor, along with whatever other matter existed in an incorporeal being. Edward wore a somewhat conceited, indifferent expression most of the time, an expression that went well with his symmetrical features and aristocratic personality. But occasionally, when he didn't realize I was looking, his face crumpled into a weary, sad frown. It was hard to imagine how difficult and frustrating it would be to have been left in a world where you no longer belonged, with no apparent relief in sight.

"Did you love her a great deal?" I realized I'd never asked the question. I'd made a vague promise to help Edward find the cause of his delay in this world, but I hadn't followed through on it.

"Who?" Edward decided Newman had had enough. His image floated up to the hearth, where he perched with his legs crossed.

His tall boots looked as black as the burnt brick in the century old hearth.

"Bonnie? The woman you fought the duel for, which I guess answers my original question. You must have loved her if you were willing to die for her."

"No, that's not necessarily true. Back in the day, when this manor was still a glittering gem, one did not say *no* to a duel. Honor was far more important than love."

"So you didn't love her? Then I suppose we can cross broken heart off the list of reasons for you not moving on."

"Love was different then too." He stared down at the tips of his boots and the earlier sadness returned. "I used dear sweet Bonnie badly. I suppose my father was right. He once told me, in one of his many stern, angry lectures, that I was not capable of love."

"I'm sorry," I said.

He looked up. "For what? That I'm not capable of love?"

"No, I'm sorry that you had a father who would tell you something so cruel and ridiculous."

It seemed the deep conversation was making him uncomfortable. His image wavered and grew dim. Aside from growing up in a time when honor was more important than love, he had grown up in a time when feelings and deep emotions were never discussed. I decided to drop the subject for the time being. But if I was ever going to figure out why Edward was stuck in limbo, I was going to need to scratch under his stony exterior and get to the heart of things.

"Well, Edward, I've had a long day. I think I'll turn in for the night."

"Good night." His tone was flat. It seemed I'd caught the inn's lingering spirit in a rare self-reflective mood. I needed to help him figure out why he was doomed to never rest in peace.

CHAPTER 19

$\mathcal{I}$ pulled the cotton quilt up over my legs and settled my back against the pillows. The house was quiet and the only sounds were Redford's soft snores and the crickets tweeting their love songs across the pastures. I moved my phone aside to reach for my book, then something occurred to me. I'd never checked the pictures I'd taken of Tory's text conversations. Since the snoop session had ended badly, with Detective Jackson catching me right in the center of it, I had apparently pushed it out of my mind. I'd only managed to catch a few back and forth texts between Brooke, Cindy and someone Tory had lovingly labeled 'Jerkface'. I doubted there would be much of significance, but I decided to check out the images I'd captured.

I swiped through to the text photos and opened up the conversation with Brooke. As I predicted, the four or five back and forth bubbles were about the bridal shower. There was no date on the picture but it was easy to tell the conversation had happened a few days before the fateful camping trip.

Brooke wrote, "Still can't decide which tent to put my cousin in. She's kind of grumpy when she's trying to sleep."

Tory responded, "Then I say make Cindy bunk with her." She punctuated her suggestion with a smiley face emoji.

"Lol, you two need to pretend to like each other. Pretty please. I'm the bride so I insist." Brooke added a heart to the end of her plea.

"Did I mention that I failed drama class? Can't pretend. I'll just try and ignore her. Got to hit the pillows. I'm beat."

"Nightie night."

I rubbed my thumb across the screen and stopped on the picture of Tory's last conversation with Cindy. At the time, I was surprised to see that Tory and Cindy had been texting at all. But as I read the texts, it became clear they rarely conversed and the tone was far from friendly. In fact, it was downright alarming.

The first text was from Tory, and it was a doozy. "I know your secret and it only confirms my hate for you."

"How did you get my new number? And you don't know anything." Cindy responded.

"Trust me, I know it all and if you don't want me to tell Brooke, then we need to talk."

"I'll just deny it. You are such a monster. Which only confirms my hate for you. Not that it needed confirmation." Cindy added another text. "I don't want to talk to you about anything. I can barely stand to look at you. No wonder everyone at Stockton Tools hates you. And delete this conversation or else."

Tory responded with a curt answer. I could almost hear an evil laugh to go along with it. "Ha, you are hardly in the position to be telling me what to do."

There was no further response from Cindy. I sat back with a deep breath. While I hadn't expected to see a jovial conversation between the two women, I had hardly expected the sharp, rage-filled chat either. Apparently Cindy had some enormous secret that she was hiding from Brooke, and Tory had somehow discovered it. She said she wanted to talk to Cindy about it. Was there some sort of blackmail in the works? The limited screenshot on my phone only allowed me to see a few inflammatory texts. The date and time weren't visible, leaving me in the dark about when the conversation had taken place. For all I knew it was from months or even a year ago. Either way, it shed some light onto just how deeply they despised each other.

I stifled a long yawn with the back of my hand. It seemed I wasn't going to be doing any reading. I had just one more conversation to look at, the one between Tory and her friend 'Jerkface'.

The first text was from Tory and she had used all caps to get her point across. "YOU ARE LATE!"

"Yeah, yeah whatever," was Jerkface's response. "One day, big deal."

Since I had no idea what Jerkface was late for, it was hard to follow the gist of the conversation. Whatever it was, Tory seemed plenty steamed by it. The last text on the page made that abundantly clear.

"You seem to forget that I am holding the one string that can unravel your entire life. TODAY or I give it a pull."

"Yeah, yeah."

Jerkface seemed to have limited vocabulary when texting. Another yawn overtook me. I put the phone aside and tried to scoot down on the mattress, a task made complicated by the placement of two sleeping dogs. I bent and turned my legs until I found a clear path to the end of the bed for my feet.

I reached over and turned out the light with only one thought left behind from the long day. Tory was not exactly a fun-loving maid of honor, and she seemed to have a few enemies.

CHAPTER 20

 rsula's shrill tone was even more grating than the shrieking buzz of Henry's electric drill. Tiny as Ursula was, she always looked big and intimidating in her oversized overalls, particularly when she was standing with her strong little fists balled up and resting on her slim hips. She was in her usual pose of standing watch over her brother Henry as he kneeled down to drill a hole for a new electrical socket. Ursula was reminding him not to get close to the old wires and letting him know that he was *turtle slow* considering he was using an electric drill. She also insisted she could get the hole drilled faster if she was twirling through the plaster with a darn toothpick. I sometimes wondered who I admired more, Ursula for being daring enough to berate a man holding a power tool or Henry for totally ignoring the high-pitched lecture raining down on him from above.

One thing was certain, I was regretting the decision to let them work on Sunday. They'd had a family event on Saturday and asked if it would be all right to finish up the electrical in the dining room on Sunday. At the time, I was just thrilled to know that they would be finishing the electrical. I hadn't considered that it meant listening to the two of them hammer, drill and yell through my entire Sunday. Normally, I was at work or out and about when they were working so I missed most of the circus. Although Edward always kindly filled me in on all the grueling details of the work day, making sure to include every argument and Ursula rant. Given Edward's naturally British accent and deep voice, he was astonishingly good at imitating Ursula's screechy tone.

"Hey, guys," I said from the doorway, deciding I was safer at a distance in case Ursula stepped on one of Henry's last nerves.

Ursula's scowl swished to a friendly grin. "Sunni, hope we didn't wake you with the drill." She motioned her head toward Henry. "Pokey here isn't very skilled with it."

Henry ignored her and kept working.

"I was thinking I'd start scraping the wallpaper in the entry-way." I pointed unnecessarily back to the entry. "What do you think?"

"Sure. That'd save us some time. I've got the perfect scraping tool right here in my tool box." Ursula was an entirely different person when she wasn't talking to her brother. She returned with a plastic handled tool that resembled a man's razor. It was topped with a sharp steel edge. "Make sure you don't touch this side," Ursula noted.

"Do you think she's some kind of dummy?" Henry asked. "Why would she touch the razor edge?"

"I'm just warning her. If you'd have gone to the safety class with me last month, you'd know that you always give out warnings where warnings are needed."

I lifted the tool with a smile. "Thanks. This should work. I'll try and make you both proud." I headed quickly out of the room.

"Someone needs to give her a warning that she's as crazy as a rabid bat," Edward uttered from behind.

"I wondered where you were at breakfast," I said without

turning back. I reached the large entryway. In its earlier days, it had been an impressive grand entry into the manor, but the tattered wallpaper and lack of a magnificent light fixture hanging from the tall ceiling made it look anything but grand.

"I was avoiding the downstairs area once those two arrived with their clamor." Edward drifted around the vast entry, looking almost lost in the house he had haunted for nearly two hundred years.

"You seem out of sorts," I noted as I surveyed the walls for the perfect starting point for wallpaper removal. Since a good third of the paper was already hanging in long shreds, I decided anywhere was a good place to start.

"I'm only out of sorts when those two are stomping about the place. Is all this really necessary?"

I looked back at him. "Uh, yes. I don't think the Cider Ridge Inn in its current state will be much of a draw for paying customers. Even freeloaders and squatters would walk past it at the moment."

"I'd forgotten that you fancy yourself an innkeeper." Edward had perfected the gentleman's scoff. It was dismissive without being vulgar and rude, and I'd heard it more often than I liked.

"That's right, I *fancy* myself exactly that. And I'm looking forward to it." I pressed the blade against the ripped edge of wallpaper and pushed the tool up the wall. Only the top layer of paper scraped away, leaving behind the thin white sticky remnants that were firmly glued to the plaster. "Huh, this might be harder than I thought."

"Why don't you wet the paper?" he suggested.

I stepped back to survey the mild damage I'd done to the wallpaper. "That's not a bad idea. Of course, it'll be much messier. But it might save me some blisters." I opened my hand and saw that the small amount of pressure on the handle had turned my palm red. "I'll get a bucket of water." Before I left the entry, I looked back at Edward. His image was faded in the morning light streaming through the string of windows running along the transom over the front door. "When did you ever take off wallpaper?"

This time his scoff had a dry laugh added to the end of it.

A knock on the front door made Edward vanish completely, but I could sense he was still in the room. I walked to the door and swung it open. "Just in time, Lana. Roll up your—" I stopped and blinked a few times to make sure I wasn't imagining the man standing on my front stoop. "Detective Jackson. I thought you were my sister." A sudden case of nerves took over. "I was going to ask her to help scrape wallpaper." I hadn't noticed my wild and exaggerated arm movements until Jackson leaned back out of the way of the sharp edged tool as it swung past his face.

I quickly pasted my arms to my sides. "Sorry, I forgot I was yielding a weapon."

Detective Jackson pushed his dark sunglasses up on his head. They nearly disappeared in his thick head of hair. "I was just up at the campsite and thought I'd stop by to see how the inn was coming." He was wearing jeans and a t-shirt but his badge was hanging on his belt.

"It's all right. It's a mess with all the work being done."

Jackson glanced back out to the driveway. "I see you've got some work going on today. The Rice siblings?"

I smiled at the way he said their name. It seemed anyone in the vicinity knew Ursula and Henry Rice. They certainly had personalities big enough to make them well known, especially in a small town.

"Yes, they're working in the dining room." Just as I finished, a loud crashing sound came from the dining room. Ursula's angry tirade followed. "Please come in. I can give you a quick tour." The initial case of nerves had subsided. I decided the only reason I'd reacted with a bit of tremble in my hands and knees was because Jackson was the last person I expected to see on my doorstep.

Jackson walked into the entry.

"I'm working on scraping wallpaper off the walls."

"That would explain nearly losing my nose to a razor blade." The sound of an unfamiliar voice in the entry brought both dogs bounding out of the kitchen. "Cool. Border Collies?" They took to him immediately, not that Redford and Newman had an ounce of snobbery in their big slobbery personalities.

"Yes. The black and white one is Newman, our tennis ball pro. And the tri-color is Redford."

"Newman and Redford," he repeated with an appreciative nod. "Well, I don't want to keep you from your wallpaper, but I thought I'd let you know we found the murder weapon in the lake."

"You did?" I had to tamp down my enthusiasm, but it was hard. Jackson was not only letting me in on a major detail in the investigation, he had gone out of his way to tell me about it.

"The hammer theory proved correct. The victim was killed with a framing hammer."

"A framing hammer?" I asked, suddenly mad at myself for not paying more attention to tools. "Is that different than a regular hammer?"

He headed toward the clamor in the dining room. "They are heavier and have a straight claw. I'm sure Henry has one in his tool box."

Ursula nearly spun right out of her giant overalls when she saw Detective Jackson walk into the room. The fake, cheery almost flirty tone that followed made it hard to stifle a laugh. It certainly brought Henry up from his crouched position.

"Detective Brady Jackson," Ursula chirruped as she glided over to meet him.

"Detective." Henry saluted him and nodded his hello.

"What brings you to the Cider Ridge Inn?" Ursula sidled up next to him. "Are you here to inspect our work? Guess they don't have enough other crimes in our town if they're sending the lead detective around for building inspections."

"Just visiting, Miss Rice," Jackson said politely. "I wonder if you have a framing hammer in that tool box? I wanted to show it to Miss Taylor."

It was hard to focus on the murder weapon when inside I was doing a happy dance about the fact that Detective Jackson had taken the time to include me on the details. Maybe I'd impressed him with my sleuthing skills after all. I would have loved to tell him about the text conversations, but since I wasn't supposed to have them, I decided to keep my lips sealed. I was certain he'd taken the phone for evidence anyhow, so he knew all about the angry text messages.

Ursula practically skipped to her tool box to retrieve the framing hammer. She handed it to him with a gracious smile, a smile I'd never seen before.

"Thanks so much." Jackson turned to me. "If you hold it you can see it's an extra heavy hammer."

I took hold of it and my hand lowered from the weight. "I guess it would take someone with a lot of strength to not only wield this but bring it down hard enough to smash a human skull." I was so giddy about being included in this sliver of his investigation that I forgot we were not alone.

"Goodness gracious." Ursula placed her hand against her chest in shock. "I may yell and scream at the man, but I've certainly never thought about hitting him in the skull with a hammer." Of course the fact that she voiced a vehement denial only made it seem more than likely that the grisly scenario of smacking her brother on the head with a hammer had occupied her daydreams more than once.

Detective Jackson seemed to come to the same conclusion as we both exchanged a secret wink. "Miss Rice, we know you wouldn't hurt your brother. I'm just using your hammer as an example for Miss Taylor." He handed it back to Ursula. She was just as anxious to put the thing away as she had been to hand it over to the detective in the first place. Our conversation seemed to have alarmed her enough that she walked over and complimented Henry on the job he was doing. Henry stared at her as if she'd grown a pair of silver horns.

Detective Jackson surveyed the work being done in the room. "This place will look great once it's done. I like working with my hands."

"I'm sure you do," Edward's distinct drawl rolled through the room. His disembodied comment stopped Jackson cold and made me nearly break into a million frozen pieces on the floor.

"What's that?" Jackson asked, looking more stunned than I felt, which was saying a lot.

I shook my head fervently. "I didn't say a word."

Jackson glanced back at Ursula and Henry. They were both deep in their respective tasks and seemingly unaware of Edward's comment.

Jackson turned back to me. I forced what I was sure was an entirely clownish fake grin.

"These walls and floors are constantly creaking and groaning. Some of the most annoying noises just come out of nowhere," I said loudly to the air, hoping a certain ghost would hear.

"Those groans and creaks sounded amazingly close to the English language." Jackson shook his head, possibly deciding he was hearing things after all.

My heart was still pumping at full pace. I decided it was time to walk the detective out. "Thanks so much for letting me know about the murder weapon. You know how I take an interest in these things."

We reached the entry where the unexpected visit had begun. It seemed the unexplained voice was still bugging Jackson. He looked back toward the room we'd just come from and stared into it for a moment. His broad shoulders rose and fell with resignation.

"Must have gotten up too early," he said more to himself than me. His extraordinary amber eyes fell back on me. "Just remember to leave the rest of the investigation to the police. Whoever did this is a dangerous person, so keep to your keyboard and let me find the killer."

Some of the earlier excitement dissipated with his warning. It made his visit even harder to explain. If he didn't want me involved in the murder, then why did he go out of his way to tell me about the murder weapon?

I nodded. "I'll keep this reporter's nose clear of any dangerous killers." I opened the door and watched his long legs carry him down the porch steps and out to his car. Then I snapped the door shut and searched around for Edward. "Smooth move there, buddy. You almost revealed yourself. And to a detective at that."

Edward's image wavered in and out of focus for a second before popping sharply into view. He drifted to the front window and watched as the detective drove away. "I spoke only to you. He should not have heard me."

"Really? Because from the look on his face, he heard every syllable."

When Edward grew defensive he could stretch his ghostly physique so that it was taller. His dark eyes gazed down at me. "I don't like him. Surely you caught the proprietary way he looked at you. As if he owned you or at the very least considers you his."

I laughed so loud it brought Ursula out from the other room. Edward stuck around, knowing only I could see him. Ursula glanced around with an expectant smile. "Did Brady leave?"

"Yes, he's gone. I'm just in here laughing to myself about what a huge task it is to scrape wallpaper."

Ursula readily accepted my excuse and went back to her work. Then it occurred to me that Ursula and Henry had not heard Edward's remark, and they had been standing in the same room.

"Why do you think Detective Jackson heard you when the words were just meant for me?"

Edward glanced back outside, but Jackson's car was long gone. "I have no idea."

CHAPTER 21

Monday or not, it was a lovely summer morning. The warm, dewy air smelled like green grass and wildflowers with the occasional dash of pine sweeping down from the mountains. I played my morning's agenda in my head several times on my drive to the *Junction Times*. I was determined to make at least one trip to Stockton Tools under the guise of writing an article about the bridge. Naturally, I'd be working on that too, but I had another better topic to cover—a murder. And since Tory had been employed by Stockton tools, I was going to be killing two of the proverbial birds with one stone. (Probably not the most appropriate metaphor for the situation but it worked.)

I turned my jeep onto Edgewood Drive, the main street that cut the commercial district in two even slices. My focus was on finding a parking spot near the newspaper office when I caught a glimpse of a familiar figure walking along the south sidewalk. It was Cindy. She looked slightly better than she had on Saturday leading me to conclude that whatever flu or virus had gripped her at the campsite was well out of her system. My mind shot back to the hate-filled text conversation between Cindy and Tory. It sure left some reason to suspect Cindy as a person of interest.

Cindy slipped quickly into the Junction Pharmacy. I grabbed the first available spot, even though it meant a three block walk to the newspaper. Suddenly, it seemed in my best investigative reporter's interest to find out what Cindy was doing in the pharmacy. It would probably contribute little toward solving the murder, but it couldn't hurt to do a touch of snooping.

The pharmacy was set up in rows of shelves. As I walked inside, I saw Cindy's bright blue t-shirt disappear around the second to last aisle. Thanks to a well organized drug store, it was easy to conclude that she was buying some kind of vitamin or food supplement. It was possible she was buying some sort of pro-biotic after her bout of stomach troubles. It seemed my mission was going to end in disappointment, but since I'd gone through the trouble of following her into the pharmacy, I decided to see it through until the end.

I stayed securely out of sight in the shoe insert aisle and busied myself with the vast array of orthopedic gels and pads. There were inserts for every level of activity. The pharmacist, a serious looking woman with thick glasses and gray hair bound tightly at the nape of her neck, finished explaining the directions for taking a medicine to an older couple. I stayed hidden in my shoe insert aisle and waited for Cindy to make her supplement selection.

The pharmacy counter was directly at the end of the aisle I stood in, but the customers faced away from me. With any luck, I'd be able to see what Cindy was buying without her seeing me. Even though I'd had little interaction with her, I could only assume she'd recognize me after spending so much time at the campsite together.

I was perusing the athletic shoe inserts when I heard the pharmacist ask, "Is that all?"

"Yes." Cindy had her black hair pulled into a ponytail. It swung back and forth as she put a box on the counter and reached into her purse for money.

I had to lean far to the right to look past Cindy's shoulder and see what the pharmacist was placing in the bag. The box was pink and had bright green lettering, but I couldn't read what the label said. I tucked a mental image of the box in my head. As Cindy turned to leave, I slipped around the back of the aisle and out of view. I turned up the vitamin and supplement aisle. For as many shoe inserts as there were, there were at least a dozen types of supplements. I scanned both sides of the aisles until the pink and green box caught my eye. I picked it up off the shelf. It seemed my mission wasn't such a disappointment after all. Cindy was buying prenatal vitamins. And unless she was buying them for someone else, which was entirely possible, that meant she was pregnant.

Suddenly, her physical state at the campsite made perfect sense. She'd been suffering morning sickness.

"Can I help you find something?" the pharmacist called from behind her counter.

"Uh no, I'm fine. Thanks." I hurried out of the pharmacy and headed toward the newspaper office.

Tory had threatened Cindy with revealing her secret. Could it be the pregnancy? And if so, why was it a secret? Possibly even more important—why was Jeremy was so attentive to Cindy on the day of the murder?

CHAPTER 22

Myrna was busy taking old flyers and advertisements off the cork board in the newspaper office when I walked inside. She was trying out a new plum colored lipstick that made the foundation on her face take on a ghoulish yellow cast. The woman loved to experiment with cosmetics, but some of the time she took the experiment a bit too far.

"Sunni, there you are. I didn't see your jeep roll past. I thought maybe you were out on assignment." She took the stack of old flyers, some of which had been posted on the board since I started the job back in April, and dumped them in the trash.

"I parked farther up Edgewood, near the pharmacy."

"I brought some of my cousin's rhubarb pie if you're interested. We had a family shindig this weekend, and there were so many leftovers, we all left with our arms full of food."

"Sounds delicious." I put my laptop down on the desk and sat in my chair. The editor's door was closed. "Is Parker meeting with

Chase?" I hadn't seen Chase since he tried to stick me with the election article.

Myrna was wearing sandals. They clacked along the tile floor as she scurried over to my desk. "Yes, they are talking about Chase covering another murder case. Apparently a woman who works for Stockton Tools was killed up at a campsite in the mountains. Not much is known yet, but Chase is preparing to head over to the police station to find out the details."

Since I had every intention of skirting right past Chase's pathetic investigative skills to find out the details on my own, I decided to keep what I knew about the murder at a minimum. Myrna had no big love or admiration for Chase, but she was good at relaying gossip to anyone who would listen.

"Yes, actually I knew about the murder. It just so happened that Lana helped plan the bridal shower camping trip for Jeremy Stockton's fiancée."

Myrna leaned her hip on the edge of my desk. "So you knew about it?" She waved her long plum colored nails. "Of course you did. Nothing gets past Sunni Taylor, crack reporter at the *Junction Times*."

I sniffled a laugh. "Yes, that's why I'm writing a story about the bridge reconstruction project and Chase is inside Parker's office laying out a plan to cover the murder."

"And we know he'll do a lackluster job of it," Myrna added. "What else do you know? Any gritty details? I suppose a murder put a quick end to the festivities."

"The actual festivities never got started. My sister will be eating chicken pot pies and s'mores for the next three months. Lana swallowed half the cost just to keep the bride-to-be's business for the actual wedding."

"Of course, I can't blame your sister. And I imagine a Stockton wedding is going to be lavish and expensive. Was it one of the guests?"

I was reluctant to share too much. "Maid of honor. Apparently she was a salesperson for Stockton Tools. Which reminds me, do you think Parker has any connections with the Stockton company? I'd like to get in to interview them about the bridge project. They are one of the large private investors."

Myrna hopped off my desk. "You're in luck then. Parker occasionally plays golf with Gary Stockton. He's semi-retired from the company now. He's put his eldest, Jeremy, in charge of things. I'm sure Parker could get you in for an interview."

Right then, Parker's office door flung open. Chase strode out looking less than enthusiastic about his new assignment. As usual he had smoothed his hair back with gel, exposing his freshly scrubbed, overly handsome face. His mouth was pulled in a straight line as he walked back to his desk with angry steps.

Parker watched him stomp off like a grumpy kid with more than a good deal of irritation. "If you're not interested, then I can hand the assignment over to Sunni."

That suggestion was all it took to change Chase's demeanor. He truly was like a child in many ways. "Nope, I'll cover the murder. I've just got a few calls, then I'm heading down to the station." He was forcing the enthusiasm, but the notion of me taking over the assignment left a sour enough taste in his mouth to make him swallow his spoiled pride.

Parker's nose was red from the man squirting far too much nasal spray into his sinuses. He insisted he had allergies, along with every other malady in the world. It seemed to give him satisfaction to be suffering from some dreaded illness, even if he was perfectly fine.

"And what are you up to, Taylor?" he asked with a gruff, nasal tone.

"Actually, I'd like a few minutes of your time if you have it." I stood up from my seat.

He motioned me into his office. I sat in the metal chair across from his desk.

Parker circled around. "I sent the article on the brewery back to your inbox. I put in a few changes but it looks good. Nice piece."

"Thank you. I'm glad. I'll put the polishing touches on it today."

Parker grabbed a cluster of used tissues from the top of his desk and tossed them into the trash. He then proceeded to smooth antibacterial lotion over his hands. "What did you want to talk about?"

I scooted forward. The tangy, pungent smell of the lotion stung my eyes. "I've got a favor to ask. I'm moving full steam ahead with the article about the Colonial Bridge."

"Good, good." He finished cleaning his hands and pulled out a new pile of tissue from the box. He mounded it on his desk. His chair squeaked as he leaned back. "What do you need from me?"

"I did some research and found that Stockton Tools is one of the private funders of the project. So I thought I'd start there. Myrna mentioned you played golf with the owner, Gary Stockton."

Parker sat forward and pulled his rolodex closer. "Sure do. In fact, I was just going to call him and see if he wanted to meet this Sunday. Not too sure though, with the tragedy this weekend and all." He squinted one eye at me. "I'll bet you already know about it."

My cheeks warmed some. "I might know a few details."

He slapped the desk, startling me and scattering his clean tissue in every direction. "I knew you would. And I'm stuck giving that walking head of bear grease the good stories. But I can get you in to see Stockton. I'll make the call right now."

"Thanks. I'm hoping to get to the bottom of the delay on the project." I got up to let him talk to his friend and make golf plans in private.

He called my name as I reached the door. I looked back at him.

"While you're over there, see what you can find out about the murder of their top salesperson."

I nodded. "I'll see what I can uncover."

CHAPTER 23

*S*omehow I imagined the main offices in the Stockton Tools Company would be far more elegant. The walls along the office hallway needed paint and the art pieces displayed between the office doors and around the waiting area looked as if they had been purchased off the back of a truck. One particular painting of a sailing ship, sitting directly across from the waiting area, looked strangely out of proportion. Dust covered fake ferns sat on laminate pedestals stationed intermittently around the reception area. A young woman sat across the way behind a tall, white counter with a headset clipped over her blonde hair as she answered numerous calls and directed them to the right extension. The leather upholstery on the waiting room chairs was worn so smooth from use, I nearly slipped right off as I sat down to wait for my meeting with the public relations manager. I was disappointed that I wouldn't be meeting with the owner, but as Parker found out from his phone call, Jeremy's father, Gary, rarely came into the office anymore.

I took great pride in my people watching skills, and as I waited for my meeting, I watched Tory's coworkers come and go. I had no idea what the usual mood was like in the office, but I'd been in enough office situations to know what a normal Monday morning atmosphere would be like. There were usually chats and quick conversations about the weekend that were punctuated by the reality that a long work week lay ahead. Monday morning was always quite dour compared to a Friday afternoon when everyone had visions of weekend plans in their heads, but I would have expected this particular morning to leave the employees in a particularly somber mood. After all, one of their coworkers had died tragically just two days earlier. It was hard to tell how close the staff was, and it was possible, but unlikely, that the office workers had little contact with the salespeople.

As I sat and waited, I pulled out my phone to check for messages. My thumb accidentally opened my reminders, which served as a reminder that I'd taken a picture of Tory's reminders. After all that reminding, I went back to the pictures I'd taken of Tory's phone and pulled up the one of her reminders. The first entry was a meeting with Sunburst Construction and the name Gilford was typed next to it. If I was interpreting the scant reminder correctly, Tory should have been at a meeting with Gilford this morning rather than stretched out on a metal table in the morgue. The next reminder was to pick up the bridal shower gift at the engraver's. The next line said 'copy behind roses, flash drive Box 673A'.

The woman answering phones took a break from her usual telephone operator tone and said 'good morning, Mr. Stockton'. My face popped up. Jeremy Stockton was standing at the counter. A leather briefcase hung from his hand, signaling he had just arrived at the office. He looked clean shaven and well groomed, as would be expected of the head of a company, but something about his attention to detail on his appearance seemed callous. A hair out of place or an extra wrinkle in his trousers would have seemed more natural on a morning just after the murder of a woman who was not only an important member of his company but a close friend of his fiancée's.

I picked up a *Country Living* magazine from the side table and lifted it in front of my face so I could turn my head and listen in on the conversation.

"I still can't believe it," the receptionist said with genuine sorrow in her voice.

"I'm just coming out of my state of shock," Jeremy said. I'd seen him for the entire morning after the discovery of the body, and I never noticed an ounce of shock. Distress maybe but shock never crossed my mind.

"Do the police know what happened?" the receptionist continued.

"Not yet. It's possible she just slipped and hit her head. One of those terrible freak accidents. Brooke insisted they have the bridal shower out under the stars. I tried to talk her out of it, but she can be hard headed."

"How is poor Brooke?" the woman asked with sincere concern.

"Seems like she'll need to find a new maid of honor before the wedding. Hey, Francine, hold all my calls for the next hour. I need to go over some numbers before I meet with the board."

"Sure thing, Mr. Stockton."

With that curt end to the conversation, Jeremy Stockton strode down the narrow hallway to the end office and walked inside. He never noticed the visitor hiding behind the magazine in his waiting area.

Shock was what I was feeling after eavesdropping on the brief conversation. Francine, the receptionist, had true sorrow in her tone as she spoke about Tory, but Jeremy's indifferent tone was nothing compared to his callous words. Speaking derogatorily about his bride-to-be as being hard headed after the woman had just lost her best friend was bad, but it was nothing compared to his flippant remark about her having to look for a new maid of honor. It was a terribly cold-hearted response. Francine didn't seem to be taken aback. It was possible that it was exactly the response she expected from her boss. It seemed Jeremy Stockton was not a nice man, and it was quite obvious that he just wasn't all that broken up about Tory's death. I was starting to wonder if anyone was distraught about Tory Jansen's murder.

CHAPTER 24

The interview with Ms. Tuttle, the head of public relations for Stockton Tools, went just as I'd expected from the woman who was the smiling, shining face of the company. Public relations people usually had one main bullet point on their job description—make the company look good no matter what the circumstances. Ms. Tuttle was great at her job.

Ms. Tuttle, a forty something woman, was wearing head to toe green, starting with a pair of green enamel clips in her hair and on through a green blazer pulled smartly shut over a green knee length skirt. The entire look was bottomed off by a sensible pair of green shoes. She never brought up one word about the recent death of a member of their sales force. Instead she bounded directly into her PR spiel about what the company did and how many store chains and independent contractors they supplied with their superior quality Stockton tools. She even had a short speech prepared about how they had been honored and thrilled to be part of the Colonial Bridge reconstruction project, making special note that they were the top private donor. Details and insignificant facts rolled over her peach pink lips. I couldn't get a question in edgewise. I was certain that was her goal. The one question I managed to blurt out—why has the reconstruction been delayed for so long—was the one inquiry for which she had no pretty speech prepared. She seemed genuinely perplexed by the delay and assured me she would check with the Junction City Council and get back to me. It seemed my trip to Stockton Tools was going to be a complete bust until she suggested a tour.

"It's very kind of you to take time out of your busy day to show me around, Ms. Tuttle," I said as I hurried to keep up with her brisk pace. We were close to skipping by the time we walked out of the offices and onto the pavement leading to the factory and warehouse. I decided to risk having the tour end early by mentioning the 'terrible news'. It was my only chance to gauge a reaction from Ms. Tuttle about Tory's death.

The employee parking lot was a vast carpet of gunmetal gray cement dotted with raised planters filled with shaggy lantana bushes. If grass took the place of the cement, it could have been a park. I found it humorous how lush the parking lot looked as compared to the shabby reception area inside the building.

We kept moving forward. It seemed my energetic tour guide was the type of person who was always moving forward, always looking ahead. I would have bet a year's salary that a seventeen-year-old Ms. Tuttle had been head cheerleader at her high school.

"For obvious reasons, insurance won't allow us to walk visitors through the factory, but you can see our warehouse and loading dock. It will give you an idea of the enormous size of our operation. And it's run like a well-oiled machine. I think you'll be impressed. In fact, you might want to make note of it for the article."

Yep, typical public relations manager. "Of course, I'll make sure to write about it. I've already heard great things about the company, and I'm sure most of the locals know just how marvelous it is." That comment caused her lips to spread wide and show brilliant white teeth. Definitely a head cheerleader's set of choppers.

My next comment erased the smile. "Again, I won't take up too much of your time. I'm sure you are quite busy this morning what with the terrible tragedy and all."

Ms. Tuttle's smooth, gliding stride faltered a bit and we slowed. She kept her focus on the warehouse ahead, but I could see her face tighten and twist as she searched for a response. When it came, it couldn't have been less informative. "Yes, well, of course. We'll keep the tour short."

The Stockton Tools warehouse was exactly what I expected, loud voices and the high-pitched warning beeps of forklifts echoing off bare industrial walls and ceilings. The endless shelving units were piled high with boxes of tools waiting to be shipped to their destinations.

I'd thrown off my sprightly tour guide with my mention of the murder. It seemed she was regretting her tour suggestion. "It's terribly noisy in here," she said loudly. "But as you can see it's a very impressive warehouse."

I let my eyes sweep around once and nodded. "Impressive indeed."

She pointed toward a back door. "The loading dock is just through there. We'll take a quick peek around, then I can escort you back to the offices."

"Great." I was about to suggest we turn around, but I didn't want to seem disinterested in the inner workings of the company. I figured the longer I stuck around, the better chance I had of stumbling onto something important. And I figured right.

Ms. Tuttle opened the door leading to the loading dock. We stepped into another vast brick building, but this one was less noisy because one side was completely open. Large rolling doors had been pushed up. Two trucks had been backed up to loading docks. And standing near a small kiosk talking to a man with a clipboard and badge that said *supervisor* was none other than Detective Jackson. They were deep in conversation.

Ms. Tuttle's phone rang, and she pulled it out of her blazer. She looked at it and grimaced slightly. "I need to take this. I'll be right back." She slipped into a small office so she could hear better. I took advantage of my short stretch of freedom and moved closer to the conversation at the kiosk.

Jackson was facing away from me and toward the supervisor. The supervisor looked too concerned with the discussion to notice a strange woman straying through his loading bay. A hammer that looked just like the one Jackson had shown me at the house was sitting on the top counter edge of the kiosk. I moved within hearing range and pretended to be enamored with the eighteen wheelers sitting in the bay. Detective Jackson was speaking just loud enough for me to hear.

"When I asked the manager of Oakley Hardware about customers who had recently purchased a framing hammer, he was surprised. He said he had just gotten a new shipment of framing hammers from Stockton Tools. There were supposed to be twelve hammers in the box, but he received only eleven. He said he called to complain."

The supervisor was a stout man with ruddy skin and heavy beard stubble. The Stockton Tools shirt was buttoned tightly across a round belly. He seemed quite thrown off by the conversation. He probably didn't normally spend his Monday morning fielding questions from a police detective. His face darkened with the question, and he reached for a messy pile of thin yellow receipts.

He cleared his throat several times as he thumbed through the papers. "As I mentioned, our foreman quit unexpectedly last week, and we've been swamped with work." He didn't look up as he spoke but continued a frantic search through the paperwork. I took the opportunity to glance toward the office where Ms. Tuttle was still occupied by her call.

My focus was pulled back to the kiosk when the supervisor cleared his throat again and said, "Oakley Hardware, here it is."

He smoothed out the semi-crumpled receipt and ran his thick finger along the bottom. "Yes, they called to let us know we shorted the order by one framing hammer." The man had dark eyes that were set a bit too close together, which only added to the flummoxed look on his face. "My signature is on the order. I always count everything before it goes out. I don't understand how I could have missed that. There are twelve slots in the carton. An empty slot would have been obvious."

"Who else has access to the warehouse?"

His rounded shoulders strained the fabric of his tight work shirt. "The warehouse employees and all the higher ups, of course."

Detective Jackson wrote something on his tablet. "One more question—"

The distinctive beeping sound of a forklift drowned out the conversation enough that Jackson paused. He turned to watch as the forklift rolled past. I scooted to the right, hoping to stay out of his line of vision. Inadvertently, I stepped over the bright yellow line showing the area to keep clear. The angry forklift driver leaned out of his seat and waved me out of the way. I stumbled back quickly and landed against a rock hard body. And there was only one of those in the warehouse at the moment.

Detective Jackson spun around quickly and grabbed me to keep me from falling. It took him a second to realize it was me. When he did, there was a twinkle in his eye that bordered somewhere between annoyed and amused.

"Bluebird. Why am I not surprised?" It took him longer than necessary to release his hold on my arms.

I brushed my hair off my face as I stepped back. "Actually, I'm here on assignment."

"Assignment," he said dryly. "Of course." He turned back to the supervisor. "Just one more question and then I'll let you get back to work." Jackson hadn't shooed me off, so I stuck around to hear the end of the conversation. "Last Thursday," Jackson continued, "I happened to be driving past Stockton Tools on my way back into town. I noticed one of your trucks pulling out from behind the loading docks. It was late, just ahead of ten."

The supervisor laughed. "That couldn't be. Our trucks always leave by six in the evening. That's when the warehouse and the loading docks close down for the night. Everyone clocks out by seven at the latest."

"There was no special order or delivery that night? Because I'm sure it was one of your trucks."

The supervisor rubbed his big fingers over his thick beard stubble to think. He shook his head. "No way. I would have been here if that was the case. Besides, Stockton doesn't like to pay overtime. With all due respect, Detective Jackson, I think you were mistaken."

Jackson nodded. "You must be right. It might have been a different truck. Thank you for your time." He turned around. We walked back through the warehouse together. Ms. Tuttle caught sight of me and waved that she'd be right out.

"So . . . were you mistaken?" I asked from the side of my mouth.

"Nope. It was a Stockton truck."

"And the hardware store was shorted a framing hammer? Was it *the* framing hammer?" I asked.

"Not sure about that yet." He stopped and turned to me. "I thought that numbskull Evans was writing the story about the murder. He came by the station this morning. I headed out the back door just to avoid him."

"Yep, Chase gets all the good stories. I'm here for an entirely different reason. Stockton Tools is a major donor for the Colonial

Bridge reconstruction project and that's the riveting piece I'm working on."

"All righty, Miss Taylor, let's skidaddle," Ms. Tuttle sing sang as she came out of the office.

"That's my tour guide, Ms. Tuttle. I think she was a cheerleader," I muttered again from the side of my mouth. "Just a journalist's instinct but I'm laying odds on not just cheer squad but head cheerleader." I stopped and flashed him my cheeriest grin. "See you later, Detective Jackson, and thanks for the extra information. I might not be writing the story but you know how I love to solve a murder."

He opened his mouth to respond, but I was whisked away by the energetic Ms. Tuttle.

CHAPTER 25

*H*alfway back to the offices, I realized Ms. Tuttle and I were not alone. Detective Jackson was walking just a few paces behind. I badly wanted to drop back and find out where he was heading next and anything else he might have discovered, but Ms. Tuttle was on her forward motion march. Once again, I was saved by her phone.

She made a tiny grunting sound as she pulled it out and looked at it. "So many fires to put out this morning." She picked up her pace.

"Don't let me keep you," I said. "I know how to get out from here. Through the office door and left at the receptionist's counter."

"Yes. Have a good day." She moved quickly ahead.

"You too. And thank you for your time." Although, I was certain I wouldn't have been given quite so much consideration if I hadn't been from the *Junction Times*.

Ms. Tuttle took a side turn to another group of offices and

entered through a locked door. I didn't need to slow my pace too much for Jackson's long strides to catch up to me.

"Where are you off to now?" he asked. "Hopefully staying clear of police business."

"Of course. You know I have no interest in police business. Just doing reporter stuff. And as a curious journalist—where is the illustrious Junction detective heading now?"

"Illustrious, huh?" His nicely chiseled jaw slid side to side. "I could get used to that one. And to answer your question sugar-coated in a compliment, I'm heading in to talk to Jeremy Stockton right now, and before you ask one of your flattering questions, you can't tag along. Even if you use all your best adjectives to describe me."

I glanced up at him as we neared the office building. "I guess I'll drop the handsome, courageous and noble idea then. I'm a journalist, so I've got quite a list up here." I pointed to my temple. "Oh, and I've got something else up in my noggin too. Something that might interest you."

We stopped a few feet short of the door and faced each other. "What is it?"

I weighed not telling him for a second but then decided it wouldn't be right to keep information from a police investigation. Besides that, he looked fairly interested in what I had to say.

I lowered my voice, just in case. "This morning on my way to work, I happened to spot Cindy Hargrove, the bridesmaid, going into the Junction Pharmacy. Guess what she was buying?"

A glimmer of a grin turned his lip up. "You were spying on her?"

"Yes. No. That's beside the point. I just happened to be checking out shoe inserts for my—for my—"

"Shoes?" he asked as his amused grin bordered on one of his sparkling white smiles.

"Yes, of course. What else would I use shoe inserts for? I was just trying to be more specific. Hiking boots," I blurted as an obvious afterthought to my lie, making it seem even more ludicrous. "Anyhow, Cindy spent some time in the vitamin aisle. Then she walked up to the counter with a bottle of *prenatal vitamins.*" I said the last two words with emphasis to make it a ta-da kind of ending. Jackson just blinked back at me with those annoyingly long lashes.

"Prenatal vitamins are supplements you take when you're pregnant," I added quickly, hoping to revive my ta-da moment.

"I know what they are. I'm just wondering why you're telling me about the trip to the pharmacy."

"Uh, because it could be very significant," I said with no small amount of irritation. "Cindy was acting strangely on the day of the murder, disappearing into the woods and emerging looking sick and pale. Which only bolsters my pregnancy theory."

"And how would you connect her pregnancy to the murder?" It was a good question. Unfortunately, I couldn't explain my reasoning without divulging my secret text photos.

"I just thought Jeremy was very attentive to Cindy, and Brooke seemed be throwing her under the proverbial bus when I talked to her."

Jackson seemed to accept my explanation. "I agree none of the bridal party was behaving the way I would have expected after one of their friends was murdered. But I'm on a more solid trail right now. That shoe print we recovered near the shrubs where Tory was killed looks to be the same brand of hiking boots Jeremy was wearing."

"That's huge. So it sounds like you have your person of interest."

He glanced around as several people walked out of the building. Once they were out of earshot, he turned back to me. "I'm not giving you an affirmative on that, and I sure don't want to see that piece of information end up in the *Junction Times*. Keep to your bridge story, and I'll keep to the homicide investigation."

"Are you sure I can't just tag along when you talk to Jeremy?"

His dark brow arched. "What do you think, Bluebird?"

"Thought it couldn't hurt to ask." We continued on toward the door. "Too bad there aren't any trees in this building. They make excellent camouflage for us nosy bluebirds."

His deep laugh rolled along the hallway toward the offices. It was a smooth, pleasing sound. Of course.

CHAPTER 26

I split off from Detective Jackson at the receptionist's desk. The exit was around the corner and down a hallway that was lined with framed pictures of the sales staff. Several bouquets of flowers were piled beneath one picture. I stopped to look at it.

Tory Jansen smiled faintly out from the posed photo. She had her hair neatly combed back, and she was wearing a white blouse and blue blazer. A small brass plate beneath her picture said, Salesperson of the Year. I glanced down at the flowers looking for some kind of message or card to snoop through, but there were only pink carnations and yellow roses.

Tom Clayborn's picture was hanging right next to Tory's. There was not one but three brass plates nailed beneath Tom's picture. He had been Salesperson of the Year three consecutive years before Tory grabbed last year's honor. I briefly mulled over jealousy as a motive for murder when the door opened and Tom Clayborn walked inside.

He was carrying a briefcase so he had either just gotten to

work or he was returning from a sales meeting. It seemed he was seeing the impromptu flower memorial for the first time. His skin tone faded to an ashy gray for a second, then he took a deep breath and shook off the apparent emotion that had overcome him. He scrutinized my face for a second, seemingly trying to remember where he'd seen me before. Then it dawned on him.

"You're with the party planner." A rightful look of confusion crossed his face. After all, why would his boss's party planner assistant show up at Stockton Tools?

"I guess we never formally met." I stuck out my hand. "Sunni Taylor."

Tom had to jam the morning's business paper under his arm holding the briefcase to shake my hand in return. "Tom Clayborn." He motioned toward his picture. "But I guess you already knew."

"Yes, I was just looking at the nice flower memorial. Terrible tragedy. Such a shocking thing to happen and in the middle of a bridal party, no less." I smiled weakly. "Although, I guess there is no un-shocking time for a young, vibrant person to die." Tom's brows knitted in confusion as I prattled on. "You're of course wondering why I'm standing in this hallway. The party planner is my sister, Lana. I just help her out sometimes. I'm actually a reporter for the *Junction Times*."

That declaration wiped away his confusion and hardened his face to anger. "My gosh, so the entire time we were being grilled by the detective, you were finding pieces of gossip to publish about the company. You reporters sure do stoop low to get a story." He ranted on, giving me no chance to step in. "Stockton Tools is a terrific company. We pride ourselves on integrity."

"Mr. Clayborn," I barked loud enough to stop his tirade. "I'm here to write a story about the Colonial Bridge project, and since Stockton Tools is a large private funder of the project, I was here to interview Ms. Tuttle."

His guilt at blowing up caused his lips to pull in as if he wished he could erase his terse lecture. "I apologize. I just assumed—"

Tom seemed sincerely sorry and contrite about it all, which made me feel guilty since my true motive for the visit was to find out details about the homicide.

"Naturally, you heard I was a reporter, so your conclusion makes perfect sense. I assure you it was just a coincidence that I happened to be at the campsite on Saturday. My sister was somewhat overwhelmed by the camping bridal shower. It was the first time she had ever had to plan an elaborate celebration in the middle of the forest."

Tom nodded. "I've no doubt of that." His eyes drifted to Tory's picture. "Of course, there was no celebration or bridal shower. Not sure how Jeremy and Brooke's wedding will proceed from here." He looked down at the flowers and then reached inside his coat and pulled out a single white rose. He placed it on top of the other flowers. "She was a cutthroat business woman and we rarely got along, but I admired her. She was a talented salesperson. The company was lucky to have her. I was lucky to work with her. I had four years experience on her, but she taught me a lot in the last year. Her loss will be felt here at Stockton Tools."

It was the first truly kind words I'd heard about Tory. "I'm sure. I can only imagine the void she leaves behind."

Tom slightly lifted his briefcase. "Well, I've got to get to work. Nice seeing you again."

"You too. Take care." I watched him turn the corner toward the offices before I headed toward the exit.

The visit to the company had been more fruitful than I'd anticipated. That was mostly due to my accidental path crossing with Detective Jackson. After listening in on some of his interview with the shipping supervisor, I'd drawn a few conclusions. It seemed Jackson was on the trail of something not above board happening in the Stockton Company, or at the very least, in the shipping warehouse. First, an order went out short a framing hammer, the weapon of choice for Tory's killer. Then there was the unexplained late night truck delivery, a delivery that the supervisor seemed to insist didn't happen. He was either lying or he really had no idea about any late night delivery. Then there was the explosive tidbit divulged by Detective Jackson that the shoe print at the scene matched the brand of shoe Jeremy was wearing. I'd also gathered some information on personal reactions to Tory's death too. It seemed Jeremy had a rather blasé attitude about it, even remarking coldly about Brooke needing a new maid of honor. A surprisingly harsh reaction. Even if Jeremy and Tory weren't close friends, she was an asset to the company. His second lead salesperson, Tom, had a much stronger and more human reaction, even though Tory was obviously his fiercest competition in the tool sales industry. And then there was Cindy's prenatal vitamin purchase. Detection Jackson blew off the information as worthless, but I wasn't so sure.

Storylines were twisting and turning, and I was continuing full steam ahead. There was nothing better than a tangled web of intrigue to get my journalistic energy roaring. I just had to figure out a way to keep close to the investigation, all the while staying clear of Detective Jackson. That wasn't going to be easy.

CHAPTER 27

*N*ick tossed the ball for Newman while Emily swept out the chicken coop. And I, being the ever-attentive aunt, played with the goats.

"What's happening at work?" Emily asked from inside the coop.

I sat down on the grass outside the coop so Tinkerbell and Cuddelbug could jump on me and nestle my hair and face. (Who needed a therapist when you had baby goats?) "I'm on a story about the Colonial Bridge project, but there's nothing too intriguing about it. After an interview with a private donor and a few calls to the city council's office, it seems the delay is more about weather and logistics than anything else."

Emily swept the debris from the coop into a pile. "What were you expecting to find?"

"Not expecting as much as hoping that there would be some sort of scandal or intrigue behind the delay. Then I would have a story. As it stands, all I have is a boring update on the progress or in this case the non-progress of the restoration plans."

Nick whistled from the pasture to get Emily's attention. "You've got an egg customer, Emi." Nick had played baseball in high school. He pitched the ball clear across the tall grass and Newman bounded after it, arcing through the tall blades and eventually disappearing in the overgrown pasture. Seconds later he emerged with the yellow ball clenched between his teeth. He was in heaven. Nick was by far his favorite ball thrower.

Emily walked out of the coop and squinted toward the road. A small yellow car turned onto the drive that led to the farm. "That's Raylene. She's a teller at Junction Bank. She stops by for a dozen eggs once a month."

Almost the second Emily had stepped out of the coop, the goats trotted to her, bleating cute little squeaks. She was their surrogate mom. I tried not to take it too personally. I stood up and brushed myself off.

"I'm going to try a new recipe for an egg salad," Emily said as we walked toward the shed where she kept the egg cartons. If it's good, we can add it to your recipe file for the bed and breakfast."

"Eggs-cellent," I chirruped with a grin.

The yellow car reached the chicken coops, and a young woman climbed out. She looked to be about Emily's age. She was still wearing her bank teller's badge on her yellow blouse. She jammed her keys in her pocket and waved to Emily as she hiked across the yard to the shed.

The goats trotted bravely forward to greet her, but once they realized she was a stranger, they bounced back to Emily for safety.

"Evening, Raylene, I thought it was about time for your egg carton."

"Yes, I'm baking a birthday cake for my mother next weekend so I needed some fresh eggs." Raylene smiled politely at me.

"Oh, silly me," Emily piped up. "Raylene, this is my sister Sunni. I was telling her that you work as a teller at the Junction Bank."

"Nice to meet you," I said. "I guess that's what happens when you rely on your phone for banking, you never get to meet the local tellers."

"So true," Raylene said. "Most of my customers are older, retired people who aren't interested in phone banking. Thanks goodness for them, otherwise I'd probably be out of a job."

"I'll put together a carton of eggs for you." Emily pointed back to her shed. "Do you still prefer a mix of medium and large?"

"Yes, six of each if you have them."

"I do." The goats followed Emily as she disappeared into the shed, leaving me outside with her customer.

"So, you're Sunni Taylor the reporter from the *Junction Times*?" Raylene asked. "I loved your story about Alder Stevens. I went to Smithville High. He was always a good friend."

"Thank you, I'm glad you enjoyed it."

"Since you're on the paper, have you heard any more about Tory Jansen's murder?"

Her question surprised me, but I jumped right into reporter mode. "Not too much yet. The police like to keep evidence close to the vest while the investigation is ongoing. Did you know Tory Jansen?" The question came out maybe a little too enthusiastically.

"Only in a business sense. She was a regular customer at the bank."

"I guess she was one of the no phone banking holdouts," I said.

"Actually, I don't know about that." She seemed to be mulling over her response. "It was strange. She came in once a week on Friday afternoon to deposit a thousand dollars cash."

"Cash deposit? I guess you don't see that too often."

"These days, almost never. And right into her personal account. But she came in every Friday at four, with the exception of this last one. She would pull a stack of twenties and fifties out of the same goldenrod envelope, and we'd chat about the usual stuff, sales at the department store, the weather, the regular. Then she'd take her deposit receipt and walk out."

"During the chats, she never mentioned what the cash was from? The sale of a car or something that might be bought with cash?"

"Never and of course I don't ask. The bank manager would frown on that."

"Of course." I thought back to Friday night when I helped Lana set up for the camping party. The bridal group, Tory included, arrived at the site around six in the evening. That would still have given her time to stop in for her regular bank deposit. "So Tory didn't come in this last Friday?"

"No but then I know she was busy with the bridal shower. She mentioned it to me the week before. Sure is tragic that she's gone. She told me she'd recently earned the title of top salesperson at Stockton Tools."

"Do you think there's any chance that the cash was from sales?"

Raylene's face blanched some at the question. "Gee, I hope not. That would be a big no-no if there was no paper trail for a company's profits." She said it in a hushed tone as if someone might be listening.

"You're right, and I'm certainly not suggesting that a company like Stockton Tools would engage in tax evasion or the likes. I'm sure there was a perfectly simple reason for Tory's weekly cash deposit."

My last comment made her mouth drop to a frown. "I guess it doesn't matter now where she got the money. May she rest in peace."

"Yes, I hope so." There was nothing more aggravating than not being able to rest in peace, I thought wryly.

Emily stepped out of the shed holding twelve brown eggs tucked into a gray carton. "I gathered these just this morning so they're extra fresh."

"Wonderful. Now if they are magical enough to make sure my mom's cake turns out right, then I'll be thrilled. There's nothing more nerve-wracking than baking for a mom who spent the last thirty years perfecting all her recipes." Raylene handed Emily money and took the eggs.

Emily winked at me. "I think Sunni and I know that mom. Our mom can bake her way out of any sort of trouble with the neighbors. She's a flour and sugar genius."

"That's true," I agreed.

Raylene nodded at me. "It was nice talking to you, and I hope they find out what happened to Tory soon. We certainly can't have a madman running around the mountain campsites killing people."

"I'm sure Detective Jackson will figure it out soon enough."

Emily and I waved as Raylene climbed into her car and drove away.

"I pulled out two plums on my visit to your farm today. Goat snuggles and, thanks to your egg customer, I'm leaving here with an interesting bit of information about the murdered maid of honor."

Emily looked over at me. "Really? What's that?"

"I'm not quite sure, but it seems Tory might have been knee deep in something illegal. She was making a thousand dollar cash deposit every Friday afternoon at the Junction Bank."

"I usually make cash deposits. Not that much and certainly not every Friday."

"Yes but you keep cash deposits in a business account so it is counted as income. Tory works for Stockton Tools. I doubt they pay salaries or commissions in cash."

"No, I'm sure they don't. That is sort of strange now that I think about it." Cuddlebug hopped up on her back legs and pushed her tiny hooves against Emily's shin, like a toddler begging to be picked up or handed a bottle.

Emily leaned down and ruffled her long ears. "It's feeding time. Would you like to—"

"Yes," I answered before she could finish. "Yes, yes."

CHAPTER 28

I started the work day not needing a new pair of shoes, but I needed an excuse to browse through Step Up Shoes in the town of Hickory Flats. Hickory Flats was a small town connected to Firefly Junction by Butternut Crest. I'd gotten to the office, slightly baffled about where to go next with the murder investigation. I resigned myself to writing a simple informational article about the Colonial Bridge, including some historical facts and a plea for the city council to get things moving on the much needed restoration project. That left me some spare time to search for clues in Tory's murder.

An hour long intense search online for any possible problems or scandals in the Stockton Tool Company proved fruitless. Other than a few disgruntled customers on Yelp, from all accounts, they were a squeaky clean, highly respected business. My disappointing search caused me to think back to the day at the campsite. I'd had an opportunity to speak to Trina, Brooke's cousin, who was more than happy to be heading back to California. The other member of the bridal party, who had mostly stayed quiet and out of the way during the initial investigation, was Kyla Forrest. I knew she had grown up next door to Brooke, which probably meant she fell into the category of friendship through proximity rather than a natural inclination for bonding. A quick call to my sister Lana and I soon discovered that Kyla worked at Step Up Shoes in Hickory Flats.

The shoe store was decorated in modern country with bright white shelves crisscrossing country blue walls. Wide planks of knotty pine covered the floors, and upholstered benches for trying on shoes finished off each shoe aisle. Kyla was no longer wearing her red hair in braids. She had it clipped up on each side, and a pair of gold hoop earrings dangled nearly to her shoulders. She was just finishing up with a customer at the register when I walked inside.

"I'll be right with you," she called from the counter.

"No hurry. I'll just look around first." I quickly made the decision that a new pair of sandals would be nice for my summer dresses. I walked over to the shelves displaying sandals and looked for a few pairs to try on. I picked up a pair that were made from a soft, supple leather.

"Those are super comfortable," Kyla said from behind. "What size?"

"Seven." I turned around and smiled.

Her blue eyes rounded. "Oh, hello. You're one of the women that works for Lana Taylor."

"Actually, I'm her sister. But I do manage to get dragged into working for her when she's busy. Unfortunately, it's all voluntary."

Kyla sighed. "Sisters. Two weeks ago I spent an entire weekend helping my sister pack up her apartment because she decided to move to the city. Three days later she called to ask if I could help her unpack because she'd changed her mind. My only reward was a pizza, and I didn't even get to pick the toppings. Seriously, who puts meatballs on a pizza? My indecisive sister, that's who."

"This sounds all too familiar to me," I agreed cheerily. It seemed we'd made an instant connection solely based on the not terribly astounding coincidence that we both had sisters. I was thrilled. It meant we could talk 'sister' to 'sister', and with any luck, I could get her to open up about the rest of the bridal party.

I turned back to the shelf and pointed out two other possible choices for sandals. Kyla hurried to the back to find my size. I sat down on a teak wood bench that was upholstered with blue and peach calico.

Kyla returned, her face hidden behind a stack of sandal boxes. She skillfully lowered the tower of boxes to the floor.

"I love the way this store is decorated," I said. "Did you do it?"

"No," she laughed. "I wish I could take credit. The owner, Milly, has great taste. I did help her pick some of the fabrics for the benches though."

I smoothed my hand over the calico upholstering. "Really cute choices." I slipped off my shoes and pulled on the nylon socks used for trying on sandals. "Have you heard from Brooke? How is she doing?"

"To be honest, I've only had a quick exchange of texts with her. She seems to be doing all right. Tory's parents are having a rough time of it, of course. But I don't know much else. I was mostly included in the wedding because our moms are good friends. Brooke and I used to hang out when we weren't busy with our own school friends. We lived just a side yard away from each other. That made impromptu play dates convenient. Our moms would have liked for us to be closer, but we just didn't mesh that well."

"Yes, I had a neighbor friend too. We'd spend a Saturday after-noon building a fort in the backyard, but we hardly said two words to each other once we were at school. Then you probably didn't know Tory well."

Kyla knelt down in front of me and threaded the leather strap on the sandal through the buckle. "Well, we did all go to the same school. I knew Cindy better than Tory. We were both in band together." She slipped my foot into the first sandal and adjusted the toe strap to fit snuggly.

"I saw Cindy yesterday morning buying vitamins at the pharmacy." I leaned over to look at the sandal. My first statement didn't get a reaction, so I decided to add the kicker. "They were prenatal vitamins."

Kyla's face shot up. "Prenatal?"

"Yes. Maybe they were for someone else," I suggested.

She focused back on the sandal and muttered something to herself.

"What?" I asked, hoping she'd repeat it.

Kyla shook her head. "It's nothing. It's just that about a month ago, I was driving along Smoky Highway on my way back from the city and I passed that crummy little motel on the side of the highway, The Great Smoky Motel, I think it's called. And I can only imagine how smoky the walls inside the rooms look. The place is so rundown, I'm surprised people stop there at all. I think it's mostly truckers who need a bed and shower. Anyhow, imagine my shock when I glanced over and saw Jeremy Stockton stepping out of one of the rooms with none other than Cindy."

I sat back hard against the upholstered seat. I was hoping to get some details about the bridal party. The last thing I expected was something so huge. "Are you sure it was them?"

"Sure as the nose on my face. I decided to push it out of my head. Like I said, Brooke and I aren't all that close. Especially not sine we've both grown up and moved away from the neighborhood. I didn't want to upset my mom by being the catalyst for some big blow up." She sat back on her knees. "Does that make me seem like a weasel? I was kind of hoping it was just some one time fling or even something innocent. Although it was hard to come up with that possible scenario. It's a really sleazy motel." She finished adjusting the second sandal.

I might not have needed them, but the new shoes were turning out to be well worth the right turn from my monthly budget.

I got up and walked around. They were comfortable and cute. I did my runway model impression and spun around on the new sandals to walk back to Kyla. She clapped her approval.

"I'll take them." I sat down to take the sandals off and put on my work shoes. "Do you think Cindy might be pregnant with Jeremy's baby?" I asked, delicately.

Kyla stood up and brushed off the knees of her pants. "It would sure explain Cindy disappearing into the forest every few minutes to get sick. I thought she'd carried some terrible flu bug with her. I've been downing all kinds of juices and vitamin C trying to get ahead of it. I guess I can't catch what she has anyhow." She laughed but stopped herself quickly. "Poor Brooke. I never did like Jeremy. Pompous, rich guy and boy, did Brooke's mom like to brag about what a 'catch' Jeremy was to my mom. Especially since I don't even have a steady boyfriend, let alone a rich one."

She carried the box of sandals to the counter. "I'm glad I haven't ordered my bridesmaid dress yet. It's expensive. I was trying to save up for it so I wouldn't have to put it on my credit card." Kyla circled behind the counter to ring up my purchase. "Maybe I'll be able to use that savings for a new pair of sandals. I've been eyeing the same pair you just bought."

It seemed slightly wicked to be talking about shoe buying at the expense of someone's happiness, but if what Kyla said was true, Brooke would be well rid of Jeremy. It would be worse to go through the chaos and expense of a wedding and then find out the truth. It seemed it was up to either the groom or the bridesmaid to come clean. I wasn't sure how any of it tied into the murder, but it definitely put a shameful spin on the entire dynamic of the wedding party.

Kyla thanked me for the purchase, and I silently and profusely thanked her for all the information. I walked out with my shoes, all the while thinking about Tory's text conversation with Cindy. Tory had threatened to reveal Cindy's *secret*. It seemed more than obvious now what that secret was, but the question remained—had Tory's threat been enough to push Cindy or even Jeremy to murder?

CHAPTER 29

*A*fter the shoe shopping excursion, I headed back to the newspaper office to hammer out the bridge article. I needed to have something for my deadline. At the same time, I wanted to get it out of the way so I could focus on the murder investigation. Chase had been in and out all morning, but something told me he wasn't any further on the article about the campsite murder than he was on day one. He tended to get easily distracted, and I was sure the police weren't handing him much information.

I reread the bridge piece and decided to close it and wait a day before revisions. Giving the story a day to rest always helped me find weak spots that needed improvement. Raine had texted that she was heading out to Lana's to work on some party decorations for a silver anniversary, and Myrna had gone out to eat with a neighbor so I was on my own for lunch. Deciding I just wasn't that hungry, I pulled a bag of trail mix out from my desk drawer and started nibbling it just as sirens screamed through town. I got up and reached the window just as Detective Jackson and two squad cars raced past.

I rushed back to my desk, grabbed my purse and ran to my jeep. The one perk about living in a small town, especially one that was a junction for all the roads leading to other towns, was that it was always easy to tell which direction police were going. Jackson and his team were heading along Crimson Grove to the Colonial Bridge. I managed to stay close enough that I could keep track of the red lights and sirens. They crossed the bridge and headed into Birch Highlands, a quiet town nestled between Firefly Junction and Smithville.

I'd only traveled through Birch Highlands a few times. The houses grew larger and more elegant as we headed deeper into town and closer to the hills bordering the mountain range. The sirens were silenced, but the red lights flashed as they disappeared around a corner and headed onto a quiet cul-de-sac of very expensive homes. There was already a squad car and a red paramedic truck parked on the street. Jackson pulled up and stopped at the end of a paved driveway that led up to a two story mansion with tall windows and a turret. Thickly clustered yellow and pink rose bushes lined the front porch. An ambulance's red lights flickered at the top of the driveway near a three car garage.

I parked. I was sure I'd hear a lecture from Detective Jackson or at least earn a scowl, but I decided to check out the situation. If it turned out, as I expected, to just be an elderly person with chest pains or hurt from a fall, then I'd scurry back to my car and head back to town, preferably without ever being seen.

I walked to the edge of the privacy hedge bordering the front lawn and peered up the driveway. My car chase through town had been worth the effort. Jeremy Stockton was sitting sideways on a gurney with a first aid ice pack pressed against the left side of his head. The paramedics were checking his eyes and his vitals. Detective Jackson stopped at the gurney to find out the status of the patient while two of his officers scanned the front yard for something.

There was no way Detective Jackson would have been called if Jeremy had just fallen or hit his head. He must have been attacked. He looked pretty shaken as he answered Jackson's questions.

The flurry of emergency people and activity on the driveway gave me an opportunity to sort of glide into the crowd and go unnoticed for a moment. I stayed somewhat camouflaged in the lush trees and landscaping adorning the front yard, but I knew it was only a matter of time before Detective Jackson spotted me sneaking around. I convinced myself to get bold and move closer to the action so I could pick up any pertinent information before being told to leave.

The uniformed officers seemed to be concentrating on a neatly trimmed laurel hedge running along the right side of the house. It was a good six feet high and at least a foot deep.

The massive trunk of a magnolia tree allowed me to stand within hearing range of the conversation at the ambulance. Jeremy's voice was shaky as he spoke to Detective Jackson.

"I was just walking to the back gate, and they jumped out from behind the hedge. The blow to my head made me black out. I never even saw the person."

"Found it," one of the officers called from the hedge. It was Officer Norton from up at the campsite. He emerged with a hammer in his gloved hand.

Detective Jackson walked with long strides over to Officer Norton. He examined the hammer. From the distance I was standing, it looked smaller than the framing hammer used to kill Tory. But still, if swung from a good angle and with good force, it could do some serious damage to a human skull. It seemed Jeremy Stockton either got lucky and missed the full force of the blow, or he had an iron hard head.

One of the paramedics walked over and said something to

Detective Jackson. He returned to the ambulance to talk with Jeremy. I remained shielded by the tree. "Mr. Stockton, since this is an assault and since it might very well be linked to the homicide case, I need you to go to the hospital for a proper examination. We've found the hammer that was most likely used to knock you out, but we need to make sure the injuries match the weapon. And if you blacked out, you really need to be checked out by a doctor anyhow."

"Yes, well I was knocked out," Jeremy answered curtly as if he thought Jackson was questioning it. "It's just I have other things to do this afternoon. As you know, I have a large company to run. I just stopped home for some lunch and to make a few phone calls. I certainly didn't expect my work day to be cut short. I've got meetings lined up for the rest of the day."

"I understand your frustration, but frankly, I think you'll be sorry if you go to work. I think once the initial shock wears off, you're going to feel that blow to your head. I can't force you, but I strongly urge you to go through a thorough examination. Otherwise it might be harder to prosecute the perpetrator."

"First you have to catch him," Jeremy barked.

"Yep," Detective Jackson said sharply. It seemed his patience was growing thin. "That's usually the way it works. You said *him*," he continued after a pause. "You didn't get a look at the person, but do you think it was a male? That would help us narrow the search."

"Why yes, or at least I assume so because of the blow to my head. Either that or a very strong woman," he said with a dry laugh.

"But you don't know for certain it was a male?"

"No, as I told you, I was out cold before I could see anyone." He sighed loudly. "I suppose I should have the doctor prescribe me some kind of pain pills. My head is starting to throb. Although, that might be more from this line of inquiry than anything else."

"Then I'll leave you alone, so you can get to the hospital. We'll be sticking around for a while longer, searching for evidence." Jackson nodded to the paramedics. They loaded their grumpy patient into the back of the ambulance.

With some of the activity slowing down and people leaving the area, I was going to be just a bit too noticeable. A group of firemen, who had shown up for the call, made their way back down to the road. I decided to trek along behind them back to my car.

"Miss Taylor?" a deep voice called from behind. I froze and waited to see if anyone else in the area stopped to answer to the same name. It seemed I was the Miss Taylor being summoned.

Detective Jackson had his hand on one hip, pushing his shirt up above the shiny badge on his belt. A faint smile appeared on his face.

I waved weakly at him. "Hello."

Jackson glanced around the yard. "Were you hiding in the trees again?"

I walked toward him. "Not *in* the trees. Just behind one." I pointed out the wide trunk of the magnolia tree.

The ambulance backed down the driveway and carried off Jeremy Stockton.

I reached the pathway where the laurel hedge had apparently served as a hiding spot for the attacker. "I saw you race past the newspaper office and I followed. What can I say? I'm a curious reporter. Besides, I have some interesting information that I think you'll want to hear."

"What is it?"

"First, a few questions about what has happened here."

He tilted his head, and darn, if it wasn't a charming look for the man. "This isn't a bartering session, Bluebird. It's a homicide investigation."

"I understand that. And for me it's a journalist's investigation."

Jackson pulled his glasses back down over his amber eyes. "I thought you were covering a story about the Colonial Bridge project."

"True. And didn't we all just cross over that bridge? I mean if that doesn't show just how important it is for the restoration to begin, then I don't know—"

"Miss Taylor," he said brusquely. "I'm in the middle of something here. What do you have on the case, or should I haul you in to the interrogation room?"

"No need for that."

Officer Norton interrupted with a question about what to label the evidence.

"Possible assault weapon," Jackson answered before turning back to me.

"I see they used a hammer," I said quickly before he could say anything. "Do you think it's the same person who killed Tory?"

He held back a grin. "Could be."

"Could be? Care to elaborate, Detective Jackson?"

"Nope."

"I guess this sort of takes Jeremy off the suspect list."

He didn't respond.

"I see. Well then, I'll tell you my information even if you're being tight-lipped."

"Good idea."

I waved my finger at him. "Just remember this point is in my column because I uncovered it."

His thick hair glistened in the sunlight coming down through the trees as he shook his head. "There are no points because this is not a game."

"Fine. Remember when you so quickly dismissed my mention of Cindy buying prenatal vitamins?"

"I didn't dismiss it. I just didn't add to it."

I pursed my lips to hold back from commenting further about his initial reaction, but I knew when I was on the receiving end of a dismissal. "Anyhow, I went into the shoe store to buy some sandals, and the salesperson just happened to be Kyla, one of the bridesmaids."

When he crossed his arms, it made the fabric on his shirt tighten across his muscles. He took off his sunglasses again. "She just happened to work there?"

"Yes. Just a big ole coincidence," I said with a quick grin. "Anyhow, I think Cindy is pregnant. She was sick the entire day at the campsite. She was weepy. She looked tired and pale with nausea, and she was buying prenatal vitamins. All those clues point to her being pregnant."

He nodded grudgingly. "And Jeremy's the father."

His unexpected response sucked the words right out of me. I stared up at him in question.

"Like I said, I didn't dismiss what you told me about the vitamins. I asked Cindy if there was anything she wanted to tell me that might affect the case. She immediately broke down in sobs about being pregnant. She didn't come right out and confess it, but it was easy to figure out that it was Jeremy's. Of course, none of this connects directly to the victim."

"Except, what if Tory knew about the secret?"

Jackson squinted down at me. "You saw Tory's phone, didn't you? When you were chasing invisible squirrels from her tent?"

I shrugged. "My eyes might have drifted over a few text messages."

"Drifted?" He rolled his eyes. "You do have a lot of interesting words in your arsenal, Bluebird. Guess that's why you're so good at your job." When we were face to face, I only came to his chest. He amplified our height difference by leaning down to look me eye to eye. "Now if you let me do my job, I can get this case solved."

"Far be it from me to stand in the way of justice, so solve away." I started to walk back to the road.

"Hey, Bluebird?"

I turned back to look at him. Somehow he always managed to look spectacular no matter where or how he was standing. "Yes?"

"That was some impressive detective work." He winked at me before turning back to his team.

I tried not to let his simple comment go to my head, but I did manage a couple skips on my way back to the car. I climbed inside and wrote a few things down on the notepad I always kept close by. The attack on Jeremy put him more on the side of victim than murderer now. But who would want to kill both Tory and Jeremy? Was Cindy capable of such a terrible crime? But why would she want to hurt Jeremy? Maybe Jeremy didn't want to tell Brooke. Maybe he told Cindy he wanted nothing to do with the baby and that she was on her own. But why kill Tory? Was Tory just a decoy for the true focus of the murder, Jeremy? And what about Brooke? It was easy to forget about her because she was the bride-to-be, and it would seem strange for her to kill her maid of honor. Brooke did seem upset with Cindy on the day of the murder. Maybe she knew all about the baby and the horrible betrayal and she was just waiting for the right time to pounce on everyone. Maybe she thought killing Tory would throw the police off the motive trail. It was all playing out like a soap opera in my head, but it was hard to know if any of my theories were even close to reality. It seemed I was going to have to burn through a lot more shoe leather to get to the bottom of this.

But not in my new sandals, they were far too cute to ruin.

CHAPTER 30

J'd stayed late in town to have dinner at Raine's house. We'd decided to make grilled cheese and tomato sandwiches with some of Emily's summer tomato crop.

I patted my stomach with a satisfied sigh. "Nothing hits the spot like a grilled cheese. I sort of just trail mixed my lunch today, so I was extra hungry." I grabbed a dry dish towel and Raine washed the plates.

"Emily's tomatoes are so delicious," Raine noted. "I've just been slicing them and eating them plain. I think she should expand her crop and start a produce stand."

"I agree. Then I could offer local farm produce at the bed and breakfast. Looking so forward to opening that place. I love journalism, but it can be tiresome, especially when I'm writing mundane articles about bridges being spit-shined."

Raine plunged her arms into a mountain of suds. "I sure hope they do more than spit-shine that old bridge. I clench my teeth tight in fear every time I drive across it. I guess that would make an interesting story, huh? Local psychic and all-around nutjob falls to her death as bridge collapses."

I took the dish from her. "Raine, no one thinks you're a nutjob."

Her laugh sent a cluster of bubbles into the air. "Yes, they do. I can't even conjure a ghost up in the most haunted place in town, the Cider Ridge Inn. Then I predict something terrible will happen from Tarot cards and when the prediction comes true, I become a suspect instead of a psychic."

"First of all, you were never a suspect. Cindy was accusing you that day because she had a huge secret she was keeping from the bride. And maybe the Cider Ridge ghost is just shy." It was one of those moments when it was nearly impossible to bite my tongue and not blurt out that there was a ghost at the inn.

Raine handed me the last dish and drained the sink. "What do you mean? What secret?"

"I'll tell you, but keep it to yourself. I haven't let Lana know anything yet because I think the Stockton wedding might be cancelled soon. I don't want to be the one to break it to my sister. I know she was excited about landing that job." I rubbed the plate dry and put it in the cupboard.

Raine grabbed some sparkling water from her refrigerator, and we sat at her little kitchen table. Her front room generally smelled too much of incense and candles because that was where she ran her psychic business. I preferred the kitchen.

"I only have circumstantial evidence, no proof, but I think Cindy is pregnant and it seems all arrows point to Jeremy Stockton as the father."

Raine sat back hard against her chair. "That would explain some of the strange stuff at the campsite on the day of the murder. I thought the groom was acting a little too chivalrous and attentive to the bridesmaid. I caught Brooke shooting Cindy a lot of icy looks the entire day. It was like high school all over again, only the main catalyst for their usual cattiness was dead. Their reactions seemed cold even for them. As you might imagine, they were not the nicest girls in high school."

"That is easy to imagine. But still, I wonder why was Brooke shooting icy looks at Cindy. She even spoke sharply about her when we were serving everyone lunch." I sipped some sparkling water and rubbed the tickle it left behind from my nose.

"Maybe Brooke knew about the baby," Raine suggested casually, but it was a brilliant suggestion.

I sat forward. "You might be right. If we were all sensing Jeremy's extra nice overtures toward Cindy, it's only logical that Brooke noticed too."

"I think there would have been a lot more chaos at the camp if Brooke had discovered the whole pregnancy scandal. Maybe she was just mad because he was paying too much attention to Cindy." Raine's phone buzzed. She grabbed it off the kitchen counter. "It's your sister."

She opened the text and read it. "Wow, what a wild coincidence." She looked up at me. "The Stockton wedding is off."

I pulled my phone out and dialed Lana. "Hey, I'm at Raine's. Why was the wedding called off?"

"Because of a typical storyline that plays out far too often. I don't know if this has anything at all to do with Tory's murder. In fact, it might be an entirely different subplot, but it seems the groom was having just a little too much fun with the bridesmaid."

"Cindy?"

Lana paused. "You already knew?"

"I've uncovered a few gritty facts. What do you know? I want to see if they match up."

"Apparently the tension and odd pairings at the campsite were due to the fact that Cindy had recently discovered that she was pregnant."

"With Jeremy's baby." I couldn't stop myself from interjecting. Lana made an irritated sound into the phone.

"Why don't you just tell it then?"

"No, sorry. Go ahead. I'll keep my big mouth shut," I promised.

"Brooke sort of tossed all the dirty laundry my way at once. We'd spent quite a bit of time together planning her wedding reception, so she seemed to feel comfortable telling me everything. Plus, it seems she's determined to ruin Jeremy's reputation."

"Who can blame her?"

"Yep," Lana agreed. "I guess it all came out as the women were gathered around the campfire. Cindy's phone was sitting on the bench when she got up to be alone in the forest. Apparently, she was having a lot of nausea. Her phone buzzed and Brooke saw a text from none other than Jeremy telling Cindy to 'keep quiet'. He sent a quick second text saying 'he wasn't ready for any of this'." Lana scoffed. "Guess he should have thought of that when he— well anyhow. The secret was sort of out. Brooke told me she was too embarrassed to tell anyone, but that night at the campfire, she confided in Tory that she thought something was going on between Jeremy and Cindy. Brooke wasn't completely sure what Jeremy was talking about, but she started getting a pretty good idea on the morning of the murder. Jeremy was certainly not hiding his feelings for Cindy. Brooke especially didn't want her cousin to know because then her aunt would know and her mom and I'm sure you get the concept of the aunt, mom phone chain. So that's it. I'm out a great party order. I'm just glad it was cancelled early. I'm still eating chicken pot pies for breakfast, lunch and dinner."

"Well, sis, I'm sorry you lost the job, but thanks for filling us in. I've been scooting around trying to solve the murder. This puts a new light on some of my theories."

Lana laughed dryly. "My sister, the amateur sleuth. Well, have fun with that. I'll see you later."

"Bye."

"I guess this time she can't blame me for the mess," Raine said. "I certainly didn't see anything about this in the cards."

"Me either. I mean, not in the cards, but in all the evidence I've been collecting. I've been briefly entertaining the notion that Tory was blackmailing Cindy about the pregnancy. It would have been a probable motive for Cindy to kill Tory."

Raine's eyes nearly popped from her head. "Do you think Cindy did it?"

"I'm not sure. If Brooke knew about the pregnancy, Tory's blackmail scheme sure would have fallen flat. Did Cindy kill Tory because she was afraid she'd tell Brooke a secret that Brooke already knew? Or maybe Tory, wanting to prove that she was the more loyal friend, confronted Cindy about the affair and Cindy got angry. But this wasn't one of those sudden murders. Who carries a hammer around at a bridal party? Tangled web indeed. And to be perfectly honest, I don't think I'm any closer to solving this mystery than I was the day of the murder."

CHAPTER 31

I'd stayed way too late at Raine's, and I'd eaten way too much. I was going to drop into bed like a sack of potatoes and sleep like a log, even with my mind swimming with possible murder and motive scenarios. As I turned onto Edgewood Drive, a large eighteen wheeler was just pulling away from Layers, probably the driver's dinner stop before heading to the highway with his load. I pulled my jeep over to let the truck pass on the narrow road. As I waited something popped into my head. Detective Jackson had seemed quite interested in the truck that he was sure he saw leaving the Stockton loading bay after business hours. I sensed that he thought there was something odd going on with the tool delivery. It was close to ten o'clock and I was dead tired, but I decided a quick detour wouldn't hurt.

I headed toward Stockton Tools. Jackson had seen a truck leaving the warehouse around ten o'clock, even though the supervisor had insisted that was impossible. I'd been focused on the interrelationships of the people at the bridal shower, but what if there was something else going on at Stockton Tools that had caused a rift between Tory and a coworker?

I figured a mild, low risk stakeout couldn't hurt. Chances were, I wouldn't see or hear anything unusual, but it was worth a try. The Stockton company took up an entire city block, and because Ms. Tuttle had been kind enough to give me a tour of the facilities, I knew that the warehouse and loading docks were at the end of that block. A wide driveway led around to the back of the warehouse, which sat adjacent to the loading dock. A tall cinder block wall lined the backside of the property, and a large sliding gate blocked anyone from driving back to the loading area.

Streetlights lit the sidewalk in front of the various buildings that made up the Stockton complex, but very few lights illuminated the parking lot and passages between the buildings. That was why an unexplained glow at the back of the property caught my interest.

On the far side of the warehouse, a small walking path led past a few lunch tables toward the back of the property. While my original intention was to sit in my car and wait to see if any trucks left the facility after hours, my curiosity just wasn't going to stand for such a staid plan. I was in the middle of an industrial area. There were very few cars and no people around. I decided on a quick jaunt to the back of the property to locate the source of the glow.

I parked my car on the opposite side of the street and walked across to the table lined pathway. It ran along a tall wall of shrubs at the end of the property. A nice lawn and flower beds had been planted around the lunch area to give the employees a scenic, peaceful break place. As I passed along between the lunch area and the building, I heard a loud gear turning sound like a truck's tailgate being lowered. A clang was followed by a few low voices. There was absolutely some activity going on behind the shipping warehouse.

I met up with the expected gate, and of course, it was locked. It was made of widely spaced wrought iron spindles. I gripped the bars and pressed my face through as far as it would go. From the angle I was at, I could only see activity when someone stepped out and away from the loading dock. I didn't know much about trucks, but the one parked at the dock was not an eighteen wheeler. It seemed to be more the size of a large furniture delivery truck. One figure stepped into the shadows, a man who I hadn't seen on my quick tour of the warehouse. He had on a dark beanie and black coat, warm gear for a summer night.

He spoke gruffly to whoever was standing out of view. "Hurry it up," he growled. "We need to get on the road."

I couldn't see farther than the last few feet of the truck, but the noises echoing across the lot seemed to indicate heavy crates were being moved. It could easily have been tools. But why was it all happening so late and under such clandestine circumstances?

I stood quietly at the gate, hidden by the shadows created by the bordering shrubs. I waited patiently, hoping I'd hear or see something that would give me more clues as to what was taking place.

Suddenly a large hand went around my mouth, stifling my scream. I was pulled back away from the gate by someone with massive arms and a rock hard chest. I tried to kick back and hit a knee or shin but no luck. My heart was pounding so hard I thought it would pop out. The hand smothered my mouth, and I struggled to breathe through my nose. My eyes watered and my mind darted to possible nightmarish scenarios of what my captor had in mind.

The man holding me lowered his head and spoke into my ear. "I'm going to let you go. But don't scream." The familiar sound of Detective Jackson's deep voice made my knees grow weak in relief. "Promise you won't scream?"

I nodded fervently.

He peeled his hand away. My heart rate began to slow from its hummingbird pace. The sheer terror of the moment had left me slightly dizzy. I took a deep breath to gain my composure. Then I turned around and threw my fist at his chin. It was like hitting a brick wall. I had to stifle a cry as I squeezed my hand against me to relieve the sharp pain.

"Ouch, ouch," I whispered loudly.

Jackson put a finger against his mouth to hush me. He grabbed my hand and led me brusquely along the path and around the shrubs. "What are you doing here?" he asked still keeping his voice low. But it was an angry low.

I shook my hand to get the feeling back. "The question is—how is your chin harder than my fist?"

Surprisingly, he took hold of my hand and looked it over. "Nothing broken. Not that you wouldn't have deserved at least a jammed knuckle."

"And the least you could do is swish your jaw side to side to show that you at least felt my punch." I gave my hand one last shake.

He crossed his arms, a gesture that always made him look even bigger than he was, if that was possible. "Why are you here?"

I was still working on my explanation, so I shot back with a question of my own. "Why are *you* here?"

He reached down and lifted the hem of his shirt to show his badge. "I'm a detective."

"Yes, I'm very aware of that. Well, I'm a reporter."

"And I'm very aware of that. And a reporter who is oblivious to danger. You shouldn't be here at night. It's not safe."

"It's fine. I just happened to be driving past Stockton Tools—"

"Late at night and on a dead end road. Makes perfect sense."

"It does. Then I saw the glow behind the—"

A truck engine started up, rattling the gate. Detective Jackson pressed his finger temporarily against my lips to shush me. He motioned for me to follow him away from the corner, where we would be seen by any truck pulling out onto the road. We crept back to the locked wrought iron gate. His height allowed him to see clearly over, but he was still at the same angle disadvantage as I had been. The truck rumbled out of the loading dock and shook the building. A loud creaking sound signaled that the gates on the driveway were opening.

"Missed it," Jackson grumbled. He scowled at me.

"That's not my fault. You were late," I hissed, trying to make a point while whispering was never easy.

"I wasn't late. I was busy dealing with the nuisance reporter who manages to show up everywhere she's not supposed to be."

Headlights lit up the street behind us. Before I could respond, Jackson hunkered down (a difficult task for someone his size) and crept back to the corner we'd just come from. He snapped a picture of the truck as it rolled toward the main road.

Jackson pointed back at me. "Stay there." He found a thin spot in the hedges and pushed through. Seconds later he popped up on the back side of the cinder block wall running behind the warehouse. He hoisted himself up and looked around, then dropped back down behind the wall. Seconds later he emerged from the shrubs, reminding me of a large grizzly bear plowing through the dense forest. I stifled a laugh.

"Don't know why you're smiling, Bluebird, but you could have gotten yourself into trouble. Whatever was happening at that loading dock tonight had nothing to do with legitimate business. You could have been in real danger if they caught you."

"I was as quiet as a mouse and everything was going swimmingly until a certain big brute scared me witless and smothered me with his giant hand."

"I didn't want you to scream and let them know we were there."

"Well, I'm not a screamer. Most of the time anyhow. I reserve the right when faced with a snake or scaly creature."

"Let's get you back on the road. It's late." Detective Jackson led me out to the street and walked me to the jeep.

"Now that we got past that awkwardness, what do you think is happening? Do you think it has to do with Tory's murder or is this a completely separate crime?"

He leaned against my jeep. "Not sure if it's related or if it's even a crime. Something seems to be leaving the warehouse past business hours. Could be something completely innocuous like hauling broken down boxes to a recycling plant."

"Only, why wouldn't the supervisor know about it?" I asked.

"Exactly. I'll have to find out. In the meantime, no more stakeouts in dark alleys."

"That lush little lunch area is hardly a dark alley."

Jackson opened his mouth to lecture me further, but I stopped it with an emphatic nod.

"I will stay away from dark alleys and stakeouts."

Jackson opened the door and I climbed inside. "By the way, nice jeep, Bluebird."

"Thanks. Till we meet again, Detective Jackson." I saluted him as he shut the door.

CHAPTER 32

"*Y*ou're late." Edward's deep voice echoed around the entryway as I stepped into the house.

"It's not even eleven and I am a grown woman," I answered without even looking around to find him. Sometimes his voice just rained down on me as if he had his own intercom speakers set up around the house.

Redford and Newman trotted out to greet me with sleepy eyes and slow wagging tails. Their late night greeting wasn't nearly as upbeat as their daytime greeting. But as I walked into the kitchen, they anticipated that I might just be heading to their treat jar. Ears and tails perked up.

I headed straight to the ceramic cat shaped canister and pulled out two dog treats. They sat obediently, something Lana had taught them, and I tossed them their cookies. They quickly carried them off to their pillows.

Edward materialized sitting on the brick hearth. "It's not safe for you to be out alone so late."

I rolled my eyes. "You sound just like Detective Jackson. Sure do have a lot of grown men butting in to my business lately."

"I'm not butting. And who is Detective Jackson?" He answered himself, saving me the effort. "Wait, that must be that cocksure fellow with the unkempt hair who visited here on Sunday. Were you out with him?"

I reached into the fridge for the carton of milk. The brief moment of terror at Stockton Tools had upset my stomach. "If I were out with Jackson, I certainly wouldn't have to tell you. Or ask permission. I'm an independent woman. You just happen to take up space in my house." I put the milk on the counter and tilted my head in question. "Or do you take up space? Are you considered matter?"

"I have no idea what that inquiry even means. You're just trying to avoid the topic."

"What topic? I'm just trying to figure out scientifically where you belong in the matter chart. Plasma? No, it can't be that. You're definitely not solid."

"If you're just going to prattle on like some old bird in a lunatic asylum, then I might as well be off."

"Nope, you're not solid. You're just gas, a lot of hot gas. So yes, billow away. I'm tired and not in the mood. Besides, I've got things on my mind other than listening to your ancient theories on my proprieties."

Rather than disappear, he moved closer. Sometimes, if he was near enough, I could almost feel a cool mist around him. Only once had we passed close enough that my hand coasted through his arm, obliterating the image and leaving my hand cool as if I'd temporarily stuck it inside the refrigerator.

I carried my glass of milk to the table and sat down. Edward took that as an invitation to hang out. He drifted over to the counter and perched. "What could possibly be more interesting or important than my ancient theories? Does it have to do with the murder investigation you've been muttering to yourself about?"

"That's called talking out loud and sorting ideas. And yes, that's what's on my mind. I'm having a hard time finding a link between the murder victim and a possible motive. It seems she was not terribly well liked by anyone, except possibly her friend Brooke. I managed to catch a few text messages on the murder victim's phone," I started but then realized I'd lost my centuries old sounding board with my phrasing. "I didn't actually catch them." I grabbed my phone from my purse. "You know how you laugh at me because I'm always tapping away on my—as you've named it— listening device? I do that to send a written message. I can also use it to take a picture of anything." I pulled up the text messages Tory had sent her contact named Jerkface. I showed them to Edward. He was still puzzled.

"What a strange way to exchange missives," he said as he squinted at the text. "Who is this, this Jerkface?" he asked.

"Not sure. But Tory, the woman who was killed with a hammer, doesn't seem to care for him. Using all capital letters on a message is considered sort of passive-aggressive."

"Passive-aggressive?" he asked.

"Showing you're angry without actually confronting the person."

"Ah yes, I've done that many times in letters. Only instead of childish capitals, I pushed extra hard on the nib. Left a nice black splotch on words I wanted to stand out. It seems to me, if you find out who this Jerkface is, you will find the killer. Blackmail is always a good motive for murder. I've been a victim of it before, and I can tell you thoughts of murder went through my head more than once."

My eyes widened. "You didn't kill the person, did you?"

He pulled down on his blue silk waistcoat sharply as if insulted.

"Certainly not. As a member of the gentry, I had a reputation to maintain."

"Yes, of course. Was that the same reputation that got you tossed onto a boat sailing to America? And exactly what were you being blackmailed for?"

Edward straightened his forever untied cravat. "Something to do with a quick, meaningless affair with the barrister's wife. Anyhow, let's return to your murder case."

I blinked at him a moment. "A barrister's wife? Yep, quite the reputation to protect." I shook my head. "I'd considered that one of the bridesmaids was trying to stop a blackmail plot because it turned out she was having an affair with the groom. Only now, I'm not so sure. The bride found out about the affair, so there wasn't much gristle there for a good case of blackmail." I read back through the texts Tory had sent to Jerkface. The last one where she said she could pull the thread that would unravel the person's life definitely sounded like blackmail. Up until the attack on Jeremy, I'd toyed with the idea that he was Jerkface. But that theory fell apart when he became a victim of the hammer wielding killer.

I swiped back to the picture of Tory's reminders. "Box 673A" I read out loud. "I've got a box at the post office, but it doesn't have any letters on it. So it can't be a mailing address box."

"You've lost me. You should go to bed. You always talk circles when you're tired. Just remember, your first instincts are usually right. At least that is what I've always found."

"Yes, but my first instincts have hit a wall. You're right, I'm tired." I got up and put my glass in the sink. "Good night, Edward."

"Good night. And don't stay out so late tomorrow night."

"It's like living with my parents again . . . only weirder," I muttered as I headed to bed.

CHAPTER 33

*I*n the early dawn hours, I'd woken with a start. My intuition or subconscious or semi-dream state, whatever it was that woke me, told me that there might very well be a connection between Tory's bank deposit and the unexplained after-hours activity at Stockton Tools. Could it be that Tory had gotten herself involved in some kind of stolen tool scheme? Or did she know too much about something that would cause the company trouble? Whatever it was, I decided to follow the money trail back to the bank.

A refund check of three dollars from my insurance company had been sitting on my stack of mail for a week. I decided to use it as an excuse to go inside the bank. With any luck, Raylene would be working. I wanted to ask her a few more questions about Tory's regular bank deposit.

Fortunately, late Wednesday morning proved to be a quiet time in the bank. On the right side of the building, two account managers sat behind desks in the area where people waited to open accounts or apply for loans. Raylene was the only teller sitting behind the counter. At the end of the teller windows was a sectioned off area that was surrounded with thick glass and a door. It seemed to be the booth for securely and privately viewing the contents of a safe deposit box because an elderly couple waited inside of it.

Raylene's face popped up behind the glass when she saw me in line. She slid open her window. "Next customer please."

I pulled the refund check from my pocket. It was a pretty silly reason to make a trip into the bank, but I had no other excuse to be there.

Raylene squinted one eye. "Wait, don't tell me. Sunni, right? It's easy to remember. Especially in summer."

"Yes, and you're Raylene. And I remembered that without even looking at the name tag."

"What can I do for you?"

"I just wanted to cash this check." I handed it to her.

She unfolded it and held back a grin. "I think we've got enough in the cash drawers to cover this."

"Great. I'll take it in small bills," I said with a wink.

I swiped my card. As she pulled up my account, another teller, a tall man with blond hair, walked out from the open safe carrying a narrow metal safe deposit box. My eyes just happened to swipe down to the box. The number was written in bold, black letters across a white field, making it easy to read. The box was labeled 358B. He continued on to the booth where the elderly couple waited.

"That's one, two, three," Raylene counted carefully as she placed each dollar on the counter. "What will you do with all this cash?" she asked with a laugh.

"Not sure yet. The possibilities are endless." I glanced around. The account managers were busy with clients, and the other teller was busy with the couple looking at their safe deposit box so I felt safe asking a few quick questions.

I tucked the money into my hand and leaned closer. "To be honest, I'm working on the murder story. I was hoping to ask you a couple of questions."

I was relieved when she looked more intrigued than taken aback. "Not sure if I know much but go ahead."

"First of all—and this one just came up—do all the safe deposit boxes have a letter at the end? For example is there a Box 673A in the safe?"

"That's easy, although I'm not sure how it connects. Every box has either an A or B after the number. Some people rent two boxes. That way they can keep the same number but have a box A and B. And the boxes go up to 1500, so there is definitely a box with that number inside the safe."

"You wouldn't by any chance know if Tory Jansen had a safe deposit box in the bank?"

She looked around, making sure she was free to speak but she kept her voice quiet. "That's easy too because I helped her open a box about three months ago. In fact, that was just before she started making her regular cash deposits."

Voices behind us signaled that one of the account managers was finished with a client and heading back to the teller area. Raylene straightened and flashed a polite smile. "Can I do anything else for you?" she asked cheerily.

The client popped back into the bank with one more question for the account manager, stopping her progress to the teller area. I decided to fire off one more question.

"You said Tory came in every Friday with a thousand dollars in an envelope, but is there a customer who comes in once a week to withdraw that sum of money?"

Her lips pulled down at the sides. I'd pushed my inquiry a little too far.

"I can't really answer that." She leaned forward. "But I can't think of anyone," she whispered quickly and straightened on her stool. "Thank you for your business and have a nice day."

"Thank you. You've been very helpful. I'll be careful not to blow this wad all in one place." I pushed the money into my purse and headed out of the bank.

I sat in the jeep and pulled out my phone to look at Tory's reminders again. The first one was a reminder about the shower gift. It was the second one that was now piquing my interest. "Copy behind roses, flash drive Box 673A," I read aloud.

I was fairly certain the box she wrote about was a safe deposit box, and if my hunch was right, it contained a flash drive. But what was on the flash drive? The first part of the reminder was even more cryptic. Copy of what? Did the flash drive contain original information for the copies? And what roses? The one place I hadn't visited yet was Tory's house. It would be easy enough to get her address.

First, my reporter's gut instinct was telling me to go back to Jeremy's house. I'd been skedaddled away from the investigation into Jeremy's attack rather quickly by Detective Jackson, but something kept sticking in my craw about the whole thing. The person who killed Tory was strong enough to kill her with one strike. Jeremy had sustained an injury, but it wasn't even close to the fatal blow Tory had received. Another thing that kept scratching at me was that the perpetrator had had enough fore-thought to ditch the weapon in the lake. It took far more effort to retrieve than the hammer that had been dropped cavalierly into the shrubs near Jeremy's house. A hammer was used for both attacks, but that seemed to be the only similarity.

I started the jeep. It was the middle of the work day so I was certain no one would be home at Jeremy's. I needed to do a replay of the attack before a quick snoop around at Tory's house.

CHAPTER 34

"ey, Myrna." The call came through my bluetooth just as I turned the corner onto Jeremy's street in Birch Highlands. "What's up?"

"Hi, Sunni, I found the address for Tory Jansen. I'll text it to your phone. Guess who just took the rest of the week off?"

"Let me guess, Chase?"

"Yep. I guess he and Rebecca are going on a cruise until next Tuesday. Must be nice. Lots of perks when you're dating the owner's daughter."

"What about his story? The case hasn't been solved. I don't imagine he has much yet." I pulled up to the curb across from Jeremy's house and parked. As predicted, there were no cars in the driveway. It looked as if no one was home.

"Chase has nothing, and Parker is plenty steamed about the whole thing."

"Well, I might just be able to step in and finish the story for him. I'm on my way to do some snooping around. Thanks for finding the address."

"Good luck and be careful."

"I will. See you soon, Myrna."

I climbed out of the jeep and hiked up the driveway. The house was set far back from the street, and the yard was so wide the neighbor's houses were both a good distance away. I walked along the pathway where Jeremy was attacked and headed to the gate he'd mentioned. The laurel hedge was thick enough to hide someone, while at the same time, pliable enough to jump through. I stuck my arm through several places to see how easy it would be surprise someone and hit them with a hammer.

I walked back toward the front of the path and then spun around to walk back to the gate. As I moved, I thought about Jeremy sitting on the gurney, looking pale and shaken and holding the ice pack against the side of his head, the left side of his head. I stopped and looked at the hedge. It was on the right, which meant the person who attacked Jeremy had jumped out of the hedge, circled around him and hit the left side of his head. All without Jeremy getting a look at him. Then the person circled back around and dropped the hammer into the laurel hedge before running off. Not a very efficient way to attack someone.

I walked back to the front of the path and glanced around the yard. A privacy hedge surrounded the front yard. The landscaping looked undisturbed. The person had either escaped along the driveway or across the front lawn and then down the driveway. As my eyes circled the yard, some pink and yellow roses caught my attention.

"Roses," I said to myself. Tory mentioned roses on her reminder. It was a farfetched idea, but since I was already there, a quick survey of the roses was in order. I just wasn't sure what I was looking for.

I walked along the front of the dozen or so bushes. Several sparrows popped out from behind a yellow bush and fluttered away in disgust that I'd disturbed their bug search. It took a little more finesse to walk behind the roses without getting scratched. The thorny branches were heavy with blossoms. The fragrance wafting up from the plants made the snoop session more pleasant, especially after it turned up nothing of interest. The gardener or landscaper had surrounded the plants with wood chips to help retain moisture and keep down weeds. All of the ground cover looked intact. The only thing surrounding the bases of the rose bushes were fallen rose petals and the occasional bird feather.

The rose search proved fruitless, but the reenactment of Jeremy's attack had certainly given me a few things to think about. Jeremy's account of the incident was taken while he was still recovering from a blow to the head. It was entirely possible he got the logistics wrong. Either that or the whole thing smelled, and not even remotely like roses.

I had one more stop on my list for the afternoon. Myrna had sent Tory's address to my phone. She lived in Smithville, the next town over. Like always, I was going in without really knowing what I was looking for, and there was a good chance that I wouldn't be able to do much more than walk around and look in a few windows. But with any luck, I'd stumble onto something that would help lead me to the end of the mystery.

CHAPTER 35

Tory's house was a cute mid-century ranch style home set on what looked to be about a quarter acre. Someone had taken the time to cover her Jaguar with a blue car cover. It sat lonely and bored in her driveway. I wondered briefly if she had paid cash for her expensive car. A chunk of change like a thousand bucks a week, apparently tax free, could go a long way in buying someone all the luxuries a person could want.

The grass on the lawn leading up to the front steps was over-grown. Tory, or perhaps a gardener, had planted pink pansies in the brick planter box running beneath the front windows. They were starting to droop from lack of water. The one thing I didn't see anywhere in the front yard were roses. It was midday, and a rather hot, humid summer day at that. With the exception of a couple of kids running through sprinklers at the end of the block, most everyone else was at work or had gone inside for the warmest part of the day. By late afternoon, a breeze would roll down off the mountains, bringing some relief to the humidity. People would come out of their houses for dog walks and bike rides. But no one would be coming out of Tory's house. It looked dark and sad, like an abandoned house.

The neighbor's dog, a poodle mix, barked once at me as I walked along the stepping stones to the back gate. It seemed to conclude I was harmless and returned to the shade in its own backyard.

I reached over and easily unlatched the back gate. The back-yard was paved with used bricks, and a nice wicker patio set sat under a large umbrella. It was sad to think just a few weeks ago Tory might have been sitting under the umbrella with her iced tea and a book, enjoying the afternoon mountain breeze. She seemed to have a nice, successful, enviable life. What on earth could she have done to get herself killed? I hoped to find some answers.

I was disappointed that there were no roses in the backyard either. It was the only clue I had to go on at the moment.

I walked up to the sliding glass door at the back of her house and pushed aside the screen. I pulled at the door, just in case, but it was locked. The afternoon sun caused enough glare that it was hard to see inside the house. I could make out the outline of a couch and chairs, but that was about the extent of my view.

I walked down the back of the house to a window where the blinds had been left open. I peered between the slats and seemed to be looking into a bedroom. The angle of the sun was less harsh on the window pane so I could see the contents of the room more clearly.

Roses. Tory's bedspread was adorned with pink roses. Could those be the roses she was talking about?

"Darn it." I was about to walk away when I doubled back to check the window. To my surprise, it slid open.

I looked around again. Even the next-door neighbor's dog had lost interest in the stranger prowling around the house. I hoisted myself up onto the ledge and hauled my legs over. My feet landed on thick, plush carpeting that looked as if it was newly installed.

Tory had definitely liked nice things. Even the rose printed bed set looked as if it had been purchased from a high quality bedding store.

I was nervous about being inside the house. I would look around and get out fast. The last thing I needed was to get arrested for breaking and entering. Not that I had to break anything because the window had been conveniently unlocked.

Twinges of guilt poked at me as I quickly ran my hands over the rose covered fabric on the bed. I had no right at all to be going through Tory's personal things, but I was certain that the reminder on her phone was an important thread in solving the case. I might just find out who killed her. I was sure she'd forgive me for touching her things if I landed the monster in jail. I would certainly do the same if I was the murder victim. If it meant finding my killer, I'd want people to tear the place apart to look for clues. Of course, I had no intention of tearing the place apart. Just a bit of harmless snooping.

I swept my hand over the bed but felt nothing of significance. I glanced quickly under the quilt, somehow convincing myself it was less of a violation if I looked fast. There was nothing. The more I thought about it, it seemed odd that someone would hide something under their bed covers. I ran my hand between the top and bottom mattress but didn't find anything except fuzzy tidbits from the mattress cover.

I decided to take a short glance around the rest of the house before leaving. After all, I'd already broken the law, I might as well make it worth the breach of protocol.

There were two more bedrooms, one made up with a nice inviting day bed and another used for storage of large items like a designer set of luggage and an antique vanity. The kitchen was decorated in red and white checks, a sort of vintage country look. My gaze circled around the room once. I was just about to leave when something caught my eye. A cute analog clock hung on the wall above the breakfast nook. Bright blue hands pointed out toward glittery silver numbers. And the entire face of the clock was bordered with a circular vine of pink roses.

I laughed to myself at how farfetched it would be that the clock roses were the roses mentioned on the reminder, but on a whim, I walked over and lifted the clock away from the wall. An envelope slid out from behind the clock and landed on my foot.

"Holy smokes." I leaned down and picked up the envelope. It contained two pictures. They were dark and blurry, apparently taken in a dark place and in a hurry. I moved toward the window where I could get a better look under the rays of sun coming through the glass.

The pictures weren't great, but they took my breath away. Jeremy Stockton was standing in what I had finally puzzled out was the loading dock at his family company. I was no gun expert, but I was certain the object he held in his hand was an assault weapon, like the kind used by soldiers. The second picture showed his face more clearly. He was placing the weapon into a large crate. A truck was parked in the loading bay, and it was dark outside. The only light came from a small portable work light that had been set up at the dock. I didn't recognize the second man in the picture.

As I pushed the pictures into the envelope, I heard a key slip into the front door. My heart skipped ahead several beats as I searched around looking for a place to hide. The person had a key, so it had to be someone who knew Tory. Her parents perhaps, or even her friend Brooke.

Loud footsteps thundered from the front room. They were too loud to belong to thin, little Brooke. The police, I thought in a panic. This time Detective Jackson would not give me a pass. I had entered a house illegally.

Then my heart skipped another few beats when the new visitor started slamming things around. It seemed whoever it was, they were searching for something. Things were being knocked off shelves in the front room. Glass shattered and heavy objects seemed to be bouncing off the walls. This was not the police or friends or a parent. I stared down at the envelope in my trembling hands. Was I holding the object of their search?

My hands shook as I shoved the envelope under my shirt and tucked it into my waistband. I tiptoed to the small pantry at the back of the kitchen. It had no door. Even if I tucked myself behind the dried goods and baskets, I'd be easily discovered.

The footsteps neared and I ducked back out of sight. The shoes pounded past the kitchen, and the same havoc began in the neighboring bedroom, Tory's bedroom. If the intruder caught me in the pantry, I'd be backed into a corner. I needed to get out of the house.

Drawers were being yanked from the dresser and tossed to the floor in the bedroom. It was my only chance. I dashed out from the pantry. As I moved, my elbow knocked a can of soup off the shelf. It hit the ground with a bang and rolled gingerly across the floor.

I made a run for the front door only to meet up with the house wrecker in the hallway. I was not surprised to see Jeremy's face, red and twisted with anger, scowling down at me.

"You," he growled. "What are you doing here?" Jeremy lunged for me. His hands grazed my shoulders as I darted away from his grasp.

The frightened tremble in my hands made it harder to open the door, but I managed to wrench it open just in time to smack his head with the edge of it. He was momentarily stunned, then roared with anger as he barreled out of the house after me. I leapt over all three front steps and landed at a run.

In my haze of terror, I became slightly aware of a siren and red flashing light. Suddenly, a car yanked into the yard and the driver's door flew open. I sobbed with relief when Detective Jackson stepped out of the car. He lifted his gun.

"Sunni, what on earth? Get behind me."

I'd never followed his directions so readily.

"On the ground, face down, Stockton," Jackson ordered. "You're under arrest for the murder of Tory Jansen."

Three police cars screeched to a halt in front of the house and a flood of officers flowed out to finish the arrest.

Jackson put his gun away and walked to where I was standing near his car. I had to fight the urge to hug him. I'd never been so glad to see anyone in my life. Only, by the look on his face, he was anything but pleased to see me. The amount of concern in his expression gave me a little hope that I wasn't in for too big of a lecture.

Then he did something I wasn't expecting. Jackson hugged me. My mind went right to thinking about how big and strong his arms were. His aftershave wasn't bad either.

"Bluebird, I ought to haul you into jail." Another unexpected reaction.

I looked up at him. He released me.

"For what?"

"Uh, where do I start the list? Trespassing? Impeding an investigation? Scaring an officer half to death?"

I squinted an eye at him. "Wait. Is that last one really a thing?"

"Maybe not but then I'm not thinking straight because of the half to death thing."

"You were worried about me?" I asked, trying hard not to read too much into it.

Jackson avoided an answer by reminding me that I hadn't answered him. "What are you doing here?"

"Instead of impeding your investigation, I was lending you a hand." I pulled the envelope out from under my shirt, a gesture that definitely had his full attention. "Before I give this to you, just know that I had nothing to do with the mess inside that house. That was all his fault." I motioned over to Jeremy who was now

189

sitting on the bottom step of the porch in handcuffs barking at the officers about wanting to call his lawyer.

I handed the envelope over. "I think he was looking for these. I think Tory was blackmailing Jeremy because she discovered that he was—"

"Running an illegal arms trade from the back of the warehouse," Jackson added before opening the envelope.

"You knew?" I asked.

His brow arched as he gazed down at me with those amber eyes. "Seriously, Bluebird, we don't all just sit around eating donuts all day. I had a tail on the truck that left the warehouse the other night. We've been collecting evidence to bring down the operation all week." He lifted the pictures. "These will help."

"Good. I think there's more."

He crossed his arms. "Oh? What else did you find out while you were supposed to be staying out of the investigation?" he asked wryly.

"Hey, I'm a reporter. Finding stuff out is my thing. Tory has a safe deposit box at the Junction Bank. I think there's a flash drive inside with more evidence."

His smile tilted. "You are quite the sleuth."

"And Tory was making a large cash deposit every Friday night, except the last Friday. You're late," I blurted without meaning to. "Jeremy is Jerkface, and he was late with the payment."

"That's right. You saw Tory's phone when you were chasing invisible squirrels." Jackson released a resigned sigh. "I should be mad but I've got to give you props for perseverance."

Officer Norton approached us. "Jax, we're ready to take him in."

"Yep, book him. I'll be in to question him soon. I just want to comb through the house."

They walked Jeremy past. Even though he was cuffed and held by two officers, I moved discretely behind Jackson's large body.

Jeremy was practically foaming at the mouth with anger as he glowered at Detective Jackson.

"You'll regret this, Jackson," he snarled. "I'll have your badge. You've got nothing on me."

Jackson lifted his chin to the officers letting them know to keep walking. They put Jeremy in the car.

"How did you know I was here?" I asked.

"I didn't. At least not until I saw your jeep when I came around the corner. We've been tracking Jeremy for two days. We were waiting for him to show up at Tory's house, so we could grab him. Figured he'd be looking for blackmail evidence."

Now I crossed my arms. "So you knew about the blackmail?"

"We seized the contents of Tory's safe deposit box two days ago. Like you said, there was a flash drive and there was even more evidence on it."

My posture deflated. "Here I thought I was cracking the case when all along you knew Jeremy was the killer."

"Not true. I didn't know for sure until Jeremy's staged attack on himself."

"Ah ha." I pointed excitedly at the left side of my head. "He claimed his attacker hit him as he came out of the hedge, but he was hit on the wrong side of his head."

Jackson looked properly impressed. "Maybe I need to add you to our team."

"Maybe. Only I seem to do all right running a parallel investigation."

"About that, Sunni." His tone grew more serious. "You could have been hurt. Stop taking so many chances."

I nodded. "Yeah, yeah, but a timid reporter never gets her story."

"Just as long as this reporter doesn't end up being the story."

I smiled up at him. "Cute play on words. Maybe you need to be on my team."

CHAPTER 36

I lowered my hands over the keyboard and started typing. "It started out as a fun camping trip slash bridal shower in the mountains. But it soon devolved into a terribly twisted murder plot that would leave one family reeling from a tragedy, break the heart of a bride-to-be and destroy the family legacy of a well-respected local business." As I paused to come up with the next line, Edward startled me by bouncing Newman's tennis ball off the wall behind my head. Newman pounced on the ball before it rolled under the stove.

"I'm working here," I said to Edward without looking up.

"You have a visitor." A knock sounded at the door the moment he finished.

"Who is it?" I asked as I got up from the table.

"It's that cocksure detective."

"Cocksure. Boy, if that isn't the kettle calling the pot black," I muttered as I headed to the front door.

Edward drifted after me. "It's not right or proper, him showing up here unannounced like this."

"Again, wrong century, Mr. Beckett." I waved him away and opened the door.

Jackson had his hair combed back off his clean shaven face. He was wearing a crisp black t-shirt and jeans.

"You look like you're off to a party or something," I noted.

He glanced down at his jeans and black boots. "Do I? No party. I was just off to see some friends."

"Come inside. Just don't look around the entryway. I'm afraid my wallpaper removal has been less than successful."

I waved him in and took a quick look around for lurking ghosts. Edward had vanished. but I was sure he wasn't far.

Jackson made the vast entryway look much smaller. Even though I'd expressly told him not to, he looked around at the walls. "It's definitely a big job."

"Bigger than I thought," I said and smiled up at him.

We gazed at each other without a word for a moment. It was hard to know what he was thinking, but I caught a sparkle in his eyes.

He finally pulled us out of the awkwardly quiet moment. "I came just to let you know that we've officially charged Jeremy with Tory's murder. Unfortunately for him, the hammer we pulled out of the water had the Stockton code number imprinted on the head. It was the missing hammer from the hardware store's order. Only a few people could have taken the hammer from the crate before it shipped."

"Sounds like you have lots of evidence to convict him on numerous crimes."

"Yes, Jeremy Stockton will never sit at the helm of his father's company. I've heard his dad is going to sell the company to help pay for legal fees."

"Nice dad. I'm not so sure I'd be that generous with my kid if he ruined the family company with his greed. And then there's the whole matter of his affair with his fiancée's good friend. Poor

Cindy. Poor Brooke. I guess some people aren't just rotten. They are *really* rotten."

"If Tory had just turned Stockton in rather than resorting to blackmail, she'd probably still be alive. Her greed got her killed." Another awkward moment followed as our gazes locked.

"Well, I've got to write the story. Frankly, I've got so much juicy stuff to mention, I'm not sure where to start. The article practically writes itself."

"I'm sure you'll put your *Sunni* spin on it." He raked his thick hair back with his fingers. The movement made his bicep curl into a ball of steel. It stretched the fabric of his t-shirt taut. "I'll let you get to work then. I look forward to reading it."

"Thanks. And thanks for filling me in on a few more details." I walked Jackson to the door. He looked back and lingered just a moment longer than necessary on the front stoop before trotting down the steps.

I turned back inside.

Edward leaned against the doorway with his arms crossed. "I don't like him."

"No one asked your opinion." I snapped the door shut and headed back to the kitchen.

ABOUT THE AUTHOR

London Lovett is the author of the Firefly Junction and Port Danby Cozy Mystery series. She loves getting caught up in a good mystery and baking delicious new treats!

Subscribe to London's newsletter [londonlovett.com] to never miss an update.

You can also join London for fun discussions, giveaways and more in her *Secret Sleuths* Facebook group.

https://www.facebook.com/groups/londonlovettssecretsleuths/

Instagram @LondonLovettWrites

https://www.londonlovett.com/
londonlovettwrites@gmail.com